A FISTFUL OF MOONLIGHT

A FISTFUL OF MOONLIGHT

New Fiction from Assam

Edited by
Mitra Phukan
Arunava Sinha
Lucy Hannah

MACLEHOSE PRESS
QUERCUS · LONDON

First published in Kolkata, India, by BEE Books in 2022
First published in Great Britain in 2023 by

MacLehose Press
An imprint of Quercus Editions Limited
Carmelite House
50 Victoria Embankment
London EC4Y 0DZ

An Hachette UK company

Project in association with

Developed through the Write Assamese project,
a collaboration between Untold https://untold-narratives.org/
and BEE Books, supported by the British Council and KfW Stiftung.

BRITISH COUNCIL   KFW STIFTUNG

'Boots', 'Roots' and 'A Wagtail's Song' were first published in English translation
in *Words Without Borders*, in December 2022

A CIP catalogue record for this book is available from the British Library.

ISBN (TPB) 978 1 52943 192 6
ISBN (Ebook) 978 1 52943 193 3

10 9 8 7 6 5 4 3 2 1

Printed and bound in Great Britain by Clays Ltd, Elcograf S.p.A.

MIX
Paper | Supporting
responsible forestry
FSC® C104740

Papers used by Quercus Books are from well-managed forests and other responsible sources

CONTENTS

EDITOR'S NOTE

Assam, the valley state in India's Northeast, has a rich heritage of storytelling, both oral and written. While the oral literature of the land continues to have a strong presence within the state through mediums such as the Ojapali performances, Assam has a written language that dates back to around the seventh century CE. The Charyapadas, which were Buddhist songs composed from the eighth to the tenth centuries, are among the earliest known writings. Among the prose writings of the past were the Buranjis of the Ahom dynasty (1228–1825), which meticulously recorded events of importance. Though initially written in the language of the Ahoms, the later entries were in Assamese. And then there was Srimanta Sankardev (1449–1568), the saint poet of Assam, whose compositions in praise of the Almighty were seminal works in a variety of genres. There were of course others too, whose work greatly enriched the fabric of written Assamese literature.

The Assamese short story can be said to have begun with Sahityarathi Lakhminath Bezbaroa (1864–1938). Before long, the form flowered in the hands of a number of literary luminaries and today the Assamese short story as a genre is acknowledged to be studded with many gems.

The stories in this anthology are a vibrant addition to this tradition. Originally written in Assamese, in translation they can stand proud in any collection. Ten of them were part of the Write Assamese project, and their writers were selected from an open call for submissions from across Assam. Three aspiring local literary translators were also selected to work alongside these writers.

There was an intensive week-long workshop with the writers and the translators in Kaziranga National Park, in the Golaghat and Nagaon districts of the state of Assam. Lucy Hannah, Arunava Sinha and I were the editorial mentors. Editorial discussions reshaped and tightened the stories and translations, until the writers as well as the translators were satisfied. This kind of workshopping was new to the participants. Indeed, the idea of a literary workshop, with writers, translators and editors working together in unison, is a new concept in the world of Assamese letters, as well. Suggestions were made, and many, though not all, were accepted and taken into account. It was an exciting experience for all involved, including the mentors. And all participants will certainly benefit from sharing ideas about writing, translation and editing that were generated during the project.

These are all contemporary stories. Ten are from emerging voices that are assured as well as sensitive to the world and the concerns around them. Some explore contemporary issues and are often a reflection of the times, while being universal in their appeal, for example, 'Roots', 'The Roar of Baghjan', and 'A Wagtail's Song'. Others are reworkings of more traditional tales, like 'Tejimola's Stepmother Found a Place to Get a Haircut', while 'The Hunt', 'Values', 'The Captive' and 'Bak: The Water Spirit', are modern classics in Assamese literature, and come from highly regarded Assamese writers.

All these stories have a strong sense of place and are rooted in the state of Assam. Together, they give the reader a glimpse of this land and its people. For it is through stories that we learn about each other. And it is through stories that we can hope to increase our understanding of our fellow human beings.

November 2022   Mitra Phukan
Guwahati, Assam

TRANSLATOR'S NOTE

The single-most important task for the three translators who have translated ten of the stories in this volume was to transfer the unique nuances and flavours of the Assamese language to English, without adding speed breakers to the reading experience.

These are challenges that all translators and translated works face, but what makes them particularly crucial is the vast gulf between the experiences of the characters in these stories and their readers. Language is the only bridge, and the translators had the immense responsibility of conveying everything gestured at, but not spelt out, in the original text to the English-language reader.

As one of the translators, Harsita Hiya, puts it, 'A primary requirement was to mould all the stories specifically for their intended audience. To adapt them via translation in a manner that conserves the beauty and voice of the source language— how each narrative feels completely at home in it—without alienating an international readership through excessive and inflexible retention of terms. This required careful navigation, as did showcasing cultural practices with exposition while steering clear of anything that came too close to spoonfeeding.'

Assamese and English are very far apart in terms of the cultural apparatus of the two languages. There was always the question of whether the intangible aspects of Assamese expressions could be accommodated in English, in a way that would be meaningful to the reader. As translator Rashmi Baruah puts it, 'An idiom or word or a particular phrase which conveys a wealth of meaning in the original language might not have an equivalent meaning in the language it is being translated into.' To ensure this emotional fidelity, these translations have been through a number of iterations, striving constantly to get closer to the original Assamese text in every respect while being written in English.

The translators were also governed by the awareness that these stories would be leaving the world in which they were conceived and written, to be read and evaluated by people around the world. In translator Syeda Shaheen Jeenat Suhailey's words, 'When a person takes on the privilege as well as the burden of translating from their vernacular mother tongue to another, perhaps to gain more participants in their world, there is an almost intrinsic sense of shame in the endeavour. One's own language should be enough, should it not?' However, as she herself answers, 'In a world that sat small and unchanging, that might have worked. But now, when all the corners of the world can be reached with ease, being able to communicate with more languages at one's disposal feels more like a victory than a betrayal.'

November 2022　　　　　　　　　　　**Arunava Sinha**
New Delhi

THE CAPTIVE

Harekrishna Deka
Translated by Mitra Phukan

He had been bicycling since afternoon. It was now almost dusk. He felt extremely tired. If only he could rest for a little while . . .

It appeared that the youth who was bicycling beside him understood what he was feeling. Suddenly raising his hand, he gestured him to a stop. The youth also got down from his own bicycle.

As he got down, he noticed the picturesque surroundings. The place was near the highlands. A stream came tumbling down from the hill and flowed past a huge rock. The sound of the brook, as it murmured and gurgled on its way, floated across to him.

Pushing his bicycle towards the rock, the youth gestured towards him, indicating that he should follow. As he neared the rock, he observed it closely. The water was bright and clear. As though a young girl from the hills had come rushing headlong down the slope, chuckling happily to herself. The simile rose, unbidden, to his mind. These days, his mind would search for metaphors and similes whenever it was confronted with something that was unfettered and unimpeded.

The youth stood on the rock, and surveyed the surroundings. He then took the bag down from his shoulders, and, looking towards him, said, 'There is no danger here. You can rest for a while.'

The word 'danger' created a strange effect in his mind. How many shades of meaning lurked behind the sense of a word! His eyes strayed to the shoulder bag that the youth had put down beside him. Even though the youth had kept its contents hidden from him, he could guess what was inside. This object inside the bag ought to have evoked fear in him. It should have been the very symbol of all that was to be feared. However, strangely enough, he ceased to worry when he heard the youth's words. Without his realising it, the youth's feeling had spread to his mind. There was no danger here, and so there was no need to be alert. Neither soldiers nor security men would come here. But, for him, what danger could there be from soldiers and security men? Was he not endangered by the contents of that bag instead? Yet, surprisingly, as soon as the youth said that there was no danger here, his mind had been emptied of all fear. And the other strange fact was that when they had been bicycling to this place, and indeed, even now, the contents of that bag imparted a sense of security, a sense of reliance, not just to the youth alone, but also to him.

As if to prove that there was no danger, the youth said,

'I am feeling quite warm. I'll have a dip in the water. Will you come?'

He was also feeling the heat. It was not yet summer. But the weather was hot, and he felt the oppressive humidity. But he did not wish to bathe at that odd hour. It would be inconvenient if he were to catch a cold or a cough. For him, as well as for the youth, it would be inconvenient. And also for the organisation to which the youth belonged. They had to change their halting places frequently.

Shaking his head, he conveyed his refusal.

The youth took out a homespun towel, a gamosa, from the bag, and plunged into the stream. The bag remained on the rock. The stream had only a moderate amount of water. Unconcernedly, the youth began to bathe.

Once more, his eyes strayed to the bag. How carelessly the youth had left it lying there! Sometimes, he was amazed. It was as though the youth and he had secretly developed some kind of understanding between themselves. The weapon inside the bag was the sign of a relationship between the youth and himself. But, for quite some time now, it was as though a change for the better had overtaken that relationship. This changed relationship was illustrated by the carelessly thrown bag. It was a portent not of danger, but of something else. He was a prisoner of faith; the youth trusted him not to attempt an escape. If he so wished, he could pick up the weapon inside the bag and escape. But he knew that he would not do so. This incident of the carelessly thrown bag seemed to change the very nature of his captivity.

There was a grassy patch beside the rock. Near it was a

tree which shaded the grass. He went to this patch of grass and lay there on his back. He thought that he would rest till the youth finished his bath. He looked at the branches of the tree above him. A beautiful bird of many colours was sitting silently on one of the branches. He remained gazing at the bird. An often-heard phrase came to his mind: 'Free as a bird'. He was not very familiar with the world of nature. He could not identify the bird. Perhaps it was a kingfisher? It had a long beak and a blue body. Perhaps there were fish in the stream. That was why the bird could not leave the place. It was bound by an invisible bond. As free as a bird!

The youth came splashing out from the water. The kingfisher suddenly took wing. Perhaps it had been frightened by the sound of the youth's footsteps.

The youth put on his clothes again. Having wrung out the wet gamosa, he put it back into the bag. He slung the bag on his shoulder, and, looking at him, said, 'Come, let us leave. We must reach the village before it gets dark.'

Both of them climbed onto their bicycles again. He rode in front, the youth followed. The hostage and his keeper. Both were now pedalling with the same idea in mind. A safe shelter from the soldiers and the security forces. It was as though he himself had arranged his own captivity. When the news of the soldiers' approach reached them, he felt the same anxiety as the youth and the others of the youth's organisation. And when they came to know that the soldiers had moved away, or when they reached a safe shelter, along with them, he, too, felt the same relief.

The narrow path became somewhat broader. This meant that their destination was not too far away now. He noticed the tracks made by bullock carts on the path. The youth's bicycle was now moving alongside his own. He looked at the youth. His face was calm and unconcerned. It was as though he was confident that there was now no possibility of either the security forces or the soldiers coming here. The unemotional state reflected in the youth's face spread to his own mind. Once more, his eyes strayed to the carelessly slung bag on the youth's shoulder. It was as though the lethal weapon inside that bag was only fulfilling a formal purpose. The weapon was no longer a harbinger of death. It was not just the sign of the relationship between the youth and himself: it was also its symbol, a symbol that expressed authority. But was it only that?

He was a prisoner at one end of the metallic gun-barrel. But, at its other end, the youth, too, was a prisoner. He suddenly remembered the kingfisher, and the phrase came to his mind again. As free as a bird! But the bird itself was bound to the water in the stream by a strange relationship. He himself was a hostage; the youth was free. But the youth could not abandon him and go away. Side by side with his own captivity, the youth, too, was a prisoner. Until he himself was free, this youth would remain a captive. The power of this lifeless gun mutely controlled their relationship.

Abruptly, the youth halted. From beside a nearby tree, two other youths came towards them. He was a little taken aback. He had not even realised that two people were standing nearby. The youth with him gestured that there was no need for alarm, which meant that the two others were also from the youth's organisation. They had a bicycle with them. The youth who had accompanied him asked them something in the ethnic tongue. He appeared to be satisfied with their reply. Once more, he climbed onto his bicycle. The youth asked him to get up on his own bicycle again; the other two also climbed on theirs. All three bicycles now began to pick up speed.

It was almost dark when they reached the village that was their destination. He saw a bamboo platform beside the path leading into the village. Some youths were sitting on this bamboo platform. They had no lethal weapons in their hands. However, they had with them a couple of stout wooden sticks. A kerosene lamp was placed in a corner of the platform. Possibly these boys were there to guard the village. The youth who had accompanied him dismounted from his bicycle and talked to them in their own language. They conveyed their agreements with nods of their heads. Sitting on their bicycles again, the youth and he pedalled towards the village. The two other youths, too, moved along beside them.

It was a tribal village in a remote area. Looking at the huts there, one could surmise that the economic condition of the villagers was far from sound. The huts had roofs of thatch and bare walls of dry reed with slits between them. It was almost dark. The villagers were busy herding their cattle together. The few people that they encountered showed no curiosity when they saw the strangers. Possibly the youth's organisation often brought people to their village in this way.

Signs of extreme poverty were visible in the huts, as well as along the paths of the village. But it looked as though the same poverty had not yet managed to affect the healthy appearance of the few people whom he saw. And the signs of acute poverty that were apparent in the other huts were not quite as visible in the hut before which they eventually halted. Actually, it was not one but two huts. A one-room hut was beside the main one. Even though its sloping roof was of thatch, its walls were attractively mud-plastered. The compound was clean, and a large storehouse was visible in a corner. There was also an indication of a large plot of cultivated land behind the house. This plot was full of jackfruit and banana plants as well as areca-nut trees and betel creepers. A stout bamboo fence encircled the house, while a bamboo gate barred the entrance.

Looking at him, the youth who had accompanied him said, 'We shall stay here tonight. This is the home of the village headman. Quite safe, in fact.'

The other two youths pushed aside the gate and, entering the compound, called out for the headman. However, the village elder had gone out and had not yet returned. His son came out of the house instead and conducted them formally into the one-roomed house in the corner.

Inside was an armless, rough-hewn chair. He was asked to sit on it. On one side of the room was a low wooden cot. Though the sheet that covered the bed was coarse, it was clean. The mild aroma of the plaster of dung and fresh earth was still in the room, which meant that the house had been cleaned not very long ago. The household had received news of their approach on this day itself. Of course, the decision to come here had been taken in haste. They usually shifted during the night. But only that morning they had come to know that a group of soldiers would reach their original hiding place that very afternoon. That was why they had fled on their bicycles in broad daylight. The news of their approach here had been conveyed this morning through a messenger.

The headman's son brought a small bucket of water along with a brass jug and a clean gamosa, and requested him to wash his hands and feet. He was taken to a corner next to the house, which was enclosed by bamboo screens. A large slab of stone was laid out in this enclosed space, so that bits of earth would not spatter around. Because it was dark already, a kerosene lamp had been hung from the bamboo screen. Looking at the still undried bamboo of the screen, he realised that these arrangements had been made for his benefit. For them, he was a visitor. Did they know, he wondered, that he was a prisoner? How could they possibly imagine that this man, who seemed to move about so freely, was actually a captive?

After washing his hands and face, he felt quite refreshed. Wiping himself thoroughly with the gamosa, he entered the room once more. This, too, was illuminated by a lamp. The youth was waiting for him there. As soon as he entered, the youth got up from his chair. Even though nothing was said, he understood that there was respect in the gesture.

Instead of sitting on the chair, he went and sat on the bed. He said to the youth, 'Sit down.'

The youth said, 'You must be very tired today. Rest. We may have to stay here for a couple of days this time. Afterwards, we shall go to a safe camp in the hills. We shall have to cross dense jungles. It will be a difficult business. So rest here for a couple of days and regain your strength.'

The youth took out two tablets from his pocket, and, offering them to him, said, 'Have these.'

He recognised them to be vitamin pills. He did not need vitamin pills for his health now, but, along with the tablets, something else seemed to come to him. Was it the warmth in the youth's gesture? Or some kind of fellow feeling? Another symbol of their relationship? He wanted to say something, but the youth went out to the verandah without waiting for his reply. He seemed to think that it was necessary only to have that silent communication between them.

As the youth left, he noticed that the bag was slung on his shoulder. It was his constant companion. The weapon gave notice of its identity from inside the bag. It was now an inert tube, the sign of the tense relationship between them.

From the verandah, the youth shouted, 'I shall remain outside.'

But he knew that the youth would not remain outside. The words said to him, in a subtle language, 'I have a duty. I shall perform that duty. But I also trust you. Don't escape from here and break that trust. My duty is inextricably linked to your cooperation.'

The youth's words, 'I shall remain outside', reminded him once more of the relationship between them. Strange, the power of these words! Even amidst the numerous opportunities for escape, these words had shackled him. But, had these words conveyed the same meaning during the first few days of his captivity? Of course, during those first few days, they had had a powerful strength of a different kind. These words had then evoked mixed feelings of fear, agitation, helplessness and insecurity.

He heard the sound of footsteps outside. A middle-aged man came into the room. He understood that this was the head of the household. A small girl followed him in. In her hands was a platter of food. He caught the whiff of cooked chicken. The headman himself had brought a jug of water. With a great deal of care, the headman placed on the floor a mat that lay in a corner of the room. He put the jug beside it, while the little girl arranged the platter on it. Formally and with humble gestures, the headman then asked him to come for his meal. The headman had brought a gamosa in his hands. This he placed on the mat.

The headman said, 'There is little in our house to offer you. Please don't mind this simple food. The news that you would be coming reached us very late. It is my good fortune that a great leader such as you is to stay in my house.'

From the headman's respectful words, it was apparent that the youth had explained his captive's identity in this manner. The headman told him to leave the platter outside the room after he had finished his meal. Turning up the lamp a little, the headman then left the room.

He was extremely hungry. Even though the rice was parboiled, it tasted quite good when he mixed it with the chicken curry. Washing his hands and face over the plate with the rest of the water in his cup, he took both and, opening the door, went out of the room. Sure enough, there were no guards outside. There was no way in which the door could be locked from the outside either. Leaving the platter in a corner of the verandah, he reentered the room and closed the door after him.

Sitting on the bed, he took out the notebook from the

satchel that he carried with him. For the last three months or so, he had been keeping this journal of his captivity. The youth had brought him this notebook when he had expressed the desire to keep a journal. Out of his total captivity of seven months, he had kept a record of his daily experiences for the last three months. He had also written down, as far as he had been able to, a record of the time before. Those entries, of course, were from memory.

As soon as he closed the door from inside, a sense of captivity engulfed him. When he closed the door, it was as though he had willingly made himself captive. He also felt as though this self-imposed captivity was normal for him. So long as the door had been open, he had not felt like this. The murmur of voices from the other house had created the impression of some link with it. That link was now severed. The room was lonely and silent. There was no opening now on any side. He felt at peace after imprisoning himself.

By not remaining there, the youth, who had said, 'I shall remain outside', had placed the prime responsibility for his own captivity on him. As long as the door was open, he had had a sense of unease. What if his mind hindered his feet from discharging that responsibility? What if his mind tempted his feet: 'The open sky is out there, there is freedom outside, go, get away!' And what if his feet really went out through the door? What if they, his feet, refused to accept the bond of that unseen trust? But no, he had shut the door. He had accepted his captivity. He had accepted the discipline of the words, 'I shall remain outside.' And the strange thing was that he felt at peace.

Rifling through the pages of the notebook, he glanced

through the previous entries before writing down the experiences of that day. It had become a habit with him to read about the events of the past almost every day. In this manner, he wished to preserve intact the memories of that time.

He had written down the experiences of the first day in the very first page of the diary. On that first day of his captivity, they had put him inside a house and locked the door from outside. 'We shall be outside, don't try to escape.' How harsh, how fearful the words had been that day! They had dragged him out from his own familiar world, and pushed him into another one. The memory of the moment made him shudder. That moment, when another vehicle had stopped before his own. Four gun-wielding youths had dragged him out from his own car, and had forcibly pushed him into the back seat of another vehicle, which had then moved ahead with great speed. That had been a terrifying moment. In a world without reason, he had experienced the danger to his very existence. Later, however, he had realised that the logic of the youths' world was not the same as the logic of reason in his own ordered existence. He had heard them say several words which he himself used, or had read. However, since he could not understand their language, those remained just gestures for him. But even those gestures had had the power to create a sense of fear in him. They also used some bookish English and Assamese words. Nation, state, revolution, imperialistic power, national consciousness, government, public, freedom, rights —in their world, the meanings of these words were completely different. The meaning of the word 'security' was also different in their world. This was because they had their own interpretation of the law. The entity that he had always thought of as a 'nation' was not, for them, a nation at all. They had created their own nation. In their eyes, his nation was an imperialist power. He had assumed that he was a citizen of a free country, but they said that he was the lackey of this imperialist power. Those laws which he had always thought of as a haven of security were perceived by them to be the means of state terrorism. Their act of kidnapping was, for him, an act of terrorism; but they viewed it as their duty to their nation. The government which he thought provided them with social and political security was for them an illegitimate government. It was, for them, but a sand bar across the mouth of a river, to be swept away by the floodwaters of revolution. He had read of many revolutions. But, with the barrels of their guns pointed at his body, these youths seemed to aim the revolution at him.

They had, of course, reassured him that he himself was quite insignificant. Their dissension was against the 'illegitimate imperialistic national power'. He had been taken hostage because he was the symbol of the repressive security arrangements of that government machinery. The national power accorded importance to symbols such as he, for that power was a repressive force. Repressive acts were carried out in the name of security. If the mask of security was lifted, that power would be revealed in its true self.

They had some demands to make of that machinery which called itself the government. (Some day, they would overthrow that power, but it would take time for the revolution to mature. Therefore, it was necessary for them to get the illegitimate government to accede to some of their demands in this way.) That other nation would grant them their demands, for it was to that imperialistic power's self-interest to have him freed. Because, if he died, the mask of security which that power used as an excuse would be ripped apart, and that power would suffer a loss of respect.

However, they had not presented their reasoning in quite that manner. But, from what he could understand of their language when they talked with each other, their logic was of this kind. He got the impression that the ideas in the world that he lived in were controlled by a kind of linguistic centre. This was as though surrounded by an electromagnetic field, which held a positive charge for him as well as for people like him who thought in the same way. The linguistic centre of these youths was also surrounded by what, for them, was a positive charge. Both of them were surrounded by positive charges from their perspectives: when both the positives approached, they repelled each other. Even with his bureaucratic attitude (he was an important government officer) he could vaguely discern that both these worlds were deeply influenced by economic realities, and this had become intermingled with politics.

And he had been afraid. He could see no escape, no way out, from the distance, the gulf between their world and his, or from the emptiness that enveloped him.

For a long time, the meaning of their words and their reasoning was hidden from him, like the words of a riddle. They did not inflict any physical torture on him at all. Though their manner of speaking was rough, they were not exactly disrespectful towards him. Once in a while, they also allowed him to exchange letters with those at home. But their ways of thinking clashed repeatedly with his own. He had not been able to trust them. He would feel as though, at any moment, the muzzles of their guns would discharge their bullets into his breast.

But even greater than this physical fear had been the tremendous mental tension he had felt. The physical hardships that he went through were, of course, quite considerable. Every day, they had to change shelters. He had no settled place to stay in. Nightly, they would wander through the fields, wade through the chest-high water of rivers, march through dense jungles and marshes. Yet he would have shrugged off these physical hardships if he had only been able to trust them. Pushing him into various rooms at night, they would stand guard outside. Occasionally, they would push him inside with the words, 'We shall remain outside. Don't try to escape.' Each word seemed weighted with ridicule, callousness and cruelty. Each word seemed to express not just his own helplessness, but also that of the national power. As it wounded him, each word became synonymous with terror.

He had been unable to comprehend how a functionary could become the symbol of the government machinery. Yet they had assumed that, by capturing him, they had unerringly dealt a devastating blow to the power of the government. They had thought that the bugle of revolution had been sounded loud and clear.

He had formed the impression that the youths were being guided by a grave error. And, like him, even the youths themselves did not understand what the outcome of that error would be.

He had not understood, either, whether the ideas in his mind were logical or erroneous. But his mistrust of the youths had grown. This mistrust also had a simple reason behind it. His guards had been changed almost every week. By the time he came to know one group of youths who guarded him, they were changed. There was no conversation between him and the youths. Only sometimes, when one or two youths who appeared to be some kind of leaders had come, only then had he had the opportunity to talk. Looking at the unemotional faces of his guards, he had been unable to fathom their thoughts. He had been unable to trust them. Just as they assumed him to be the symbol of the government, he, too, had thought of each one of them as a diminutive symbol of terrorism.

But four months ago, everything had changed. The change had seemed to come from the very day that this youth had come and taken charge. Even within their own positive magnetic fields, both had seemed to discover small negative charges also. This had allowed their two minds to meet.

He did not know whether or not the youth was part of the higher echelons of power. But it was apparent that the youth was not just an ordinary guard. For, on many occasions, he took independent decisions without waiting for orders from above. The youth's pronunciation of English words had given him the impression that he was highly educated. Though of a different ethnicity, he spoke Assamese fluently. They talked mostly of everyday matters. Sometimes, however, each of them expressed their opinions and talked of their ideals. The youth professed deep faith in their revolution, but would listen attentively to what he himself had to say. There was never any callousness or disregard in his words.

On the very first day that the youth had taken charge, he had made an arrangement that had seemed to change the very nature of his captivity. Till then, the door had always been locked from outside after he had been put into a room. When the guards were nearby, they had always trained their guns at him. This youth had had no gun in his hands on the first day when he had come to him. He had not brought along other guards either. He had enquired into his well-being, and had also given him news of his family. As he was leaving, he had said, 'Latch the door from inside. I shall be outside. Don't be afraid.' He had gently shut the door behind him.

'Don't be afraid.' These words had had a strange affect on him. The emptiness, the sense of discord that he had felt all these days, seemed to vanish in a moment. Because the words 'Don't be afraid' followed them, the meaning of the sentence 'I shall be outside', too, had seemed to change. The difference between the two sentences 'Don't try to escape' and 'Don't be afraid' seemed to represent two completely different ways of viewing the same situation.

However, the other circumstances remained unchanged. He had to be shifted frequently from one place to another. They had moved from village to village at night, stung by mosquitoes and bugs. There was no question of staying anywhere for any length of time. For the organisation that the youth belonged to believed in always being in a state of extreme alertness. The change was in his own mental condition. He was a hostage, the youth was his keeper. Yet, somehow, without them being aware of it, this relationship had now changed. In spite of the difference in their ages, there developed between them a bond of companionship.

The youth had never behaved like a guard. Certainly, he always carried a gun in his bag. No doubt, the gun was the sign of their relationship, but that sign had undergone a basic change. From a sign of terror, it had become a sign of trust.

And so, while wandering on their journeys from village to village, through hills and valleys, sometimes he was the youth's teacher, while the youth was his disciple. Every now and again, the youth would mention some famous writer. At these times, the fact that he was very well read had been a great help. He had been happy to be able to talk about those writers and their work. The youth then listened to him like an attentive student. But when the subjects were those relating to nature, rural life, agriculture, farming and so on, the youth became the teacher, and he the student. He had no clear idea about the relationship between man and nature. In a strange way, this life of captivity helped him to augment the store of knowledge that he had had in his state of freedom.

After reaching a village, on one occasion, he had fallen seriously ill. The high fever made him pass out several times. Even in his semi-conscious state, he had been aware that the youth had secretly gone and fetched a doctor from a distant city. On becoming conscious, he had seen the youth sitting beside his bed. On his face there had been an expression of great anxiety. When the fever had finally subsided, he had come to know from the head of that household that the youth had not stirred from his side until he came round. The youth had given him his medicines, heated water for him, sponged down his body, put cold compresses on his forehead and had even cleaned up his excrement, all in an astonishingly compassionate way. However, the youth had not expressed any emotion after he had recovered. He had merely said, 'Your family was not informed of your illness. They would have been worried. Hope you don't mind.' He had mumbled his gratitude.

After his fever had subsided, they had had to remain for quite some time in the same village till he had recovered his strength. During this period, the two of them had discussed a variety of topics. At that time, he had expressed a desire to keep a journal. He had thought that the youth would not agree to his keeping an account of his captivity. But the youth had readily agreed, and had brought him a notebook the very next day. After writing down his entries, he would always show them to the youth, who would read them. Sometimes, the youth would nod his head, as though he had been able to catch a glimpse of his soul through these entries in his journal. After his illness, he had felt a greater sense of uncertainty. His conscious mind had not been aware of this. But the youth, reading aloud from his journal, had pointed out to him how the uncertainty of his subconscious mind was revealed in these entries.

After he had gained some strength, it was necessary once more for the youth to change their halting places frequently. Sometimes, while pondering on the uncertainty of his ever being freed, he would become restless. This would be reflected in his journal.

One day, while reading these entries, the youth had said, 'You are impatient to be free, aren't you? But look, your government is not concerned about you at all. We have sent them some terms and conditions. We can release you as soon as those conditions are met.'

He had asked, 'And if they don't agree to your terms?'

On hearing his question, the youth was at a loss for words. After a while, he had said with a smile, 'In that case, you will have to become one of us. Would you mind?'

In the end, he had stopped thinking of freedom. He had accepted his captivity as the normal condition of his life now.

Around this time, the youth had relaxed the vigilance that surrounded his captivity. After saying, 'I shall be outside', the youth would go somewhere else instead of standing guard outside. From the very beginning, the youth had always carried his gun around unobtrusively, so that it had remained invisible to him. Sometimes, he would leave the bag containing the gun lying near him. It seemed as though, without any outward sign, the youth was giving him numerous opportunities to escape. But, on the other hand, even in the midst of these unlimited opportunities, the youth had seemed to bind him to himself with an invisible bond.

Around this time, also, the news that groups of soldiers, as well as the police, were searching these areas thoroughly for him, had begun to trickle in. But he had not viewed these bits of information as something to be happy about. When news of the soldiers' approach would reach them, he, too, would become anxious. His mind, too, would clamour to go with the youth to a place of 'safety'. A part of his conscious mind understood that this kind of behaviour would be considered illogical by everybody in his own world. Even then, whenever he heard of the approach of the soldiers seeking to free him, he would think of safety as a distance between those soldiers and himself. Safety, for him, was the gun in the youth's hands.

Even today, when they received the news of the approach of soldiers, they had immediately fled to the shelter of this village. After settling him down in this room, the youth had gone off somewhere else, perhaps to the main house, to sleep. And, in the meantime, he had latched the door and accepted his captivity willingly.

As on other days, now, too, he wrote down the events of the day. Swallowing the two tablets that the youth had given him with a draught of water, he lay down on the rough bed. The safety of the bed seemed to embrace him.

He woke at dawn to the sound of birdsong. Unlatching the door, he went out to the verandah. The head of the household seemed to have been waiting for him to emerge from his room. With much ceremony, he brought a cane stool and, placing it in the verandah, requested him to sit on it. The little girl, who had brought him his food the previous night, now brought him a bowl of black tea along with molasses. The others of the family appeared to be keeping a respectful distance from the 'leader'. Even though there was no milk in the tea, he quite enjoyed sipping it from the bowl along with the molasses.

The two youths who had brought them here the previous

evening now appeared on the bicycle. They looked around for the youth who was his guard. On hearing their voices, the youth came out from the other house. They informed him at once that this place was no longer safe. They had met some soldiers just a few kilometres away. The soldiers had stopped and searched them, and had asked them if they knew whether some strangers had come this way. They, however, had sent the soldiers in the direction of a distant village.

Listening to them, the youth said, 'We shall have to move camp today. These villages are not safe anymore.'

For some time now, he had been on the verge of asking the youth a question. Because of a sense of hesitation in his mind, it had remained unasked. But, today, he abruptly questioned, 'What will you do if the soldiers surround the house and try to rescue me?'

The youth seemed unprepared for this sudden question. He did not answer immediately, but remained staring at him. After a while, the youth asked softly in return, 'Tell me, what will you do?'

This question in reply to his own startled him. He did not know how to reply.

The youth continued, 'If those circumstances arise, I shall have no choice but to execute you.'

On hearing this, he remained staring dazedly at the youth's face. This same youth had nursed him devotedly to health through a serious illness, yet he was now talking quite unconcernedly of executing him!

The youth seemed to understand his feelings. He said, 'You are not our enemy. But don't have any illusions. A government seeks legitimacy by protecting its citizens. But we have to prove that your government cannot ensure the safety of its citizens. Your death will not be caused by me, or by our organisation. Your government will be the cause of your death. If our revolution is to succeed, it will be my duty to kill you if those circumstances arise.'

Strange logic! He knew that no law of any country would ever accept this logic as just. But, in the youth's world, it was this logic that had entrenched itself. He felt that the youth had no alternative but to take this stand. The thought of his own execution had caused an upheaval in his mind. But this upheaval now subsided. He felt quite calm. He seemed to leave his own sphere of logic and step into the youth's world. Even the words 'revolution', 'legality', 'justice' and so on acquired different meanings in this other world.

It was decided that they would begin their journey to the camp that very evening.

In the meantime, the youth sent off some village lads to check the safety of the route along which they were to travel. One of these boys brought back devastating news while they were having their afternoon meal. The soldiers had, in the meantime, searched out the camp, and had destroyed it that morning. There was, therefore, no question of going there now. Even though this hamlet was no longer as safe as it had been before, they would have to spend the night here. Tomorrow, they would move again in search of a place of safety.

The youth busied himself in strengthening the security arrangements for the night. Just before dusk, several new faces appeared. He got a hint of their weapons inside their bags. The youth who was his guard gave them many instructions and they went off in various directions to guard the paths entering the village. The youth also sent the headman and his family to another house for the night.

The youth said to him, 'We shall make special arrangements for this night. For your own safety, I shall have to spend the night in your room. Several of our Freedom Fighters will stand guard around the house. If we can see this night through, we can go to another place in the morning.'

From the youth's words, he understood that the 'Freedom Fighters' had come to this village to secure his captivity.

They had their evening meal even before it grew dark. After a while, darkness engulfed the surroundings. The youth was with him in the dim lamplight of the room. The silent, lonely surroundings seemed to throb. The youth did not speak. Extremely alert, he remained standing beside the door. Today, he carried the lethal weapon in his hand openly. He himself remained sitting motionless on the bed.

Looking at him, the youth said, 'Go to sleep. I shall remain awake.'

But he remained sitting where he was. Even if he wished to sleep, would sleep come to him this night?

Perhaps he dozed. He woke up with a start when one of the youths who stood guard outside banged the door and entered the room. This boy said something to the youth who guarded him. He then went out again, shutting the door behind him.

The youth said, 'The enemy has surrounded us on all sides.' He looked at the youth. Their eyes met. The youth's gaze was steady and unblinking. He now gestured to him to leave the bed and come forward.

He heard some explosions outside. He realised that the

sounds were not those of crackers. They were the sounds of gunfire. He got down from the bed and stood before the youth.

The youth trained the gun at his breast.

He realised that the final moment of his captivity had arrived. Could the final moment be this long!

Just then, he heard the sounds of several guns being fired at the same time. He thought, 'So, this is what death is like.'

But why was he still conscious?

Everything seemed to happen at once. He saw great gobs of blood gushing from the youth's mouth. His body was riddled with bullets. The gun slid from his hand, and his lifeless body crashed to the ground like a felled tree.

The final moment of his captivity had not turned into the moment of his death. For the youth had not fired his gun. He had lowered it instead. And, at that very moment, countless bullets had crashed into the youth's body.

Several soldiers rushed into the room. One of them extended his hand towards him. He said, 'Captain Batra. Thank God! You are safe.'

Captain Batra had an RT set in his hands. The instrument crackled, Captain Batra spoke into it: 'Operation successful. Target safe. One terrorist killed.'

Terrorist! The word crashed against the magnetic centre in his skull, where it exploded loudly. Two words seemed to drag themselves agonisingly out of his mouth, 'Aaah, no!'

He sat beside the lifeless body of the youth. Placing his hand on his cold forehead, he remained staring at the youth's open, lifeless eyes.

Captain Batra did not stop him. Standing beside the dead body, Captain Batra paid his formal respects by touching his cap with his hand.

TEJIMOLA'S STEPMOTHER FOUND A PLACE TO GET A HAIRCUT

Manaswinee Mahanta

Translated by Harsita Hiya

Once upon a time, Tejimola's stepmother used to have a name. Yet, like many other women her age, she could no longer recall what it was. Other women at least acquired new identities after their marriage. Daughter of a family, daughter-in-law of another, wife of Mr XYZ and so on—all these identities were inextricably tied to these women, and even one of them was enough to erase any sign of their own names. But Tejimola's stepmother didn't have any of these. Just like the merchant's cruel new wife in the old Assamese folktale, she had no identity left in this world except for the title of stepmother.

Tejimola's stepmother.

She giggled as she bathed the puppies of the building's stray dog who had recently had another litter. As if the title was worth anything. All the same, she couldn't deny its existence. She wiped the puppies down with an old towel and pushed them towards the light to dry under the sun. The searing August heat of Guwahati, topped by the hunger pangs of high noon, sent them rushing straight to their mother's feeding bowl, whining and whimpering. Not yet old enough to eat solid food, but look at the little gluttons, she thought to herself.

She left the courtyard and went back inside. Washing her hands, she entered the kitchen and poured out some milk from the saucepan into an old, damaged glass. She took it out and left it in a bowl for the puppies, who licked it clean in minutes. Then they gathered around her, nipping and pulling at the hem of her long tunic with their tiny nails and as yet toothless mouths. Tejimola's stepmother crouched on the floor and began petting them.

Who was she to these puppies, she wondered.

This was yet another relationship which had given her no name. They recognised her certainly, but not by her name. Had she ever been tied to anyone? Had she known a relationship she could hold higher than her name? As far as human bonds were concerned, she was still fairly detached. She had her parents, yes. Her elder sister too—although it was hard to say how much of her was left since she had taken her husband's name. There was an uncle from her father's side. A distant relative who lived in the same town, a regular guest at their house. Years ago, she recalled how this man, twenty-two years older than her, had bribed her two-and-a-half-year-old self with chocolates. Unknown to the rest of the family, he had tried to build a relationship of another kind with her.

Tejimola's stepmother had spent her days gasping for

air. She grew up recoiling from her own body. Her very eyes revolted in disgust whenever the man showed up at their house. She was unable to do her chores, and pots and pans kept crashing to the floor, although no one heard, no one understood, no one knew—not even her mother. The relationship continued until her wedding with the merchant, during unexpected power cuts and on days when no one else was at home. Another relationship without a name. On some days she was called a whore; on others, a slut. She had never asked for any of these epithets, not wished for them in secret. Perhaps when a relationship is imposed for such a long time, freeing oneself is impossible. That a scream itself is enough to break such shackles was something she did not understand, not until she gave up her own name to become Tejimola's stepmother.

Another nameless association had once lurked for her on the way to college. The man, known to all as Bohua, was a newcomer to their remote town—he had come to help the merchant inspect his tea gardens in the area. One day, he thrust a letter into her hands and disappeared behind a royal poinciana. She only learnt his real name upon opening the letter. Shakya Sourav.

What twist in the tale, what bend in the road, had caused a beautiful name like this to be cast aside in favour of the one that meant 'joker'?

The thought left her fidgeting, but she did not see the man again. He had disappeared from the college road before she could muster the courage to reciprocate his overtures. He disappeared just when she thought she had found someone to share the many things she longed to share.

Soon afterwards, a group of women arrived from the merchant's house bearing a tray of gifts for her, a pile of new mekhela sadors woven with large, beautiful motifs—kingkhap, kolka, gosa, mogor and so on. She used a string to make the ancestral ring they had given her fit tightly around her finger. At nineteen, she married the forty-one-year-old merchant, becoming mother to a twelve-year-old Tejimola. Hardly a mother. Stepmother was more like it.

After about ten days of their marriage, the merchant asked her to bring out refreshments for Bohua, who was visiting them at the time. Bohua couldn't stop praising the tea she had served that afternoon. He nodded in agreement with the merchant who declared that even if there were a thousand helpers, it needed a woman to run a household. Yes, a nineteen-year-old woman was certainly needed to tend to a twelve-year-old, he agreed readily. When he stood up to leave after the snacks, she appeared outside to present him with a handwoven gamusa, which rendered him speechless. Had she handed it to him as a mere gift for a guest, or did the gamusa carry the weight of the day he had disappeared behind the royal poinciana? Bohua was left wondering. The same evening—or perhaps it had been a few days later; days and weeks were lately fuzzy in her memory—someone slid a piece of paper beneath the front door of their flat. She had just lit an earthen lamp and begun moving through the rooms with the incense when she spotted the note. She peeped through the eyehole, spotting a man running off with a familiar gamusa covering his face in spite of the blazing heat of July. The merchant had gone to Silpukhuri to attend to business. She picked up the piece of paper which had come without a seal or an envelope. Reading it explained to her the cowardice of a man who had lived all his life under the merchant's protection. She tore up the letter at once and got rid of it in the toilet, flushing away, along with its pieces, the man called Shakya Sourav from her life. Yet she was unable to discard the letter he had given her before she had ever worn a wedding ring, not to forget the notes she had scribbled in her diary about him back when he had suddenly vanished. She hid these valuables in a corner of her cupboard amidst her clothes, just like the fragrance of the ketaki petals she had once found concealed in her grandmother's trunk.

Though she was brought in to oversee the household, Tejimola's stepmother didn't have much to do in her new home, apart from washing her hands before meals. She wasn't allowed any excuse, occasion or opportunity to do things her way in the merchant's house. There was no need to work in the kitchen or give instructions to the cook. The gardener personally tended to even the money plant sitting on the double-door fridge. She had no choice but to spend her time in self-care—grooming her eyebrows, keeping her tresses shiny at the spa, working out to stay lean but curvy in the gym, having almonds to make her skin glow, preventing acne with margosa face packs and so on. Despite having a thousand other things to see to, the merchant made it a point to accompany her on trips to buy clothes—a merchant's wife had to dazzle, after all. She needed to catch the eye of society with her wardrobe, just like Tejimola's mother in the past. Dazzle, yes, but only from a distance, though, which was why the merchant carefully picked out all her outfits. One day, after she cooked her mother's recipe of pork curry with bamboo shoot, the cook informed her that sir and Teji Aaiti didn't eat pork. She put the curry out for the dog. She did not remember who threw away the bamboo shoots. Thankfully, no one stopped her from feeding the dog.

Six months after her wedding, news arrived one midnight from the merchant's ancestral home in Kohora. Bohua had been trampled to death by an elephant. The merchant himself was in Kolkata at the time. The elephant's mother had been given away to the forest department back when the merchant's father was still alive. Ever since, the animals had only visited the old house to feed on jackfruits and banana plants. And, once a year, for the religious rituals of Ganesh Chaturthi. No one had questioned why Bohua had approached the elephant at midnight. No one had wondered why the elephant, who otherwise only ever visited during the day, had shown up at the house so late without his groom. Afterwards, people didn't even ask why an animal capable of such violence was still allowed to carry people around on his back. Without these questions ever being raised in any court of law, the news eventually faded away. Of course, not long before the incident, Tejimola's stepmother's diaries had mysteriously disappeared from her cupboard, even though the letter had been left where it was. In the days that followed, she had looked at her husband with suspicion in her eyes.

Over meals. During tea on the terrace. Even while he shaved.

But there was nothing unusual about the merchant's behaviour. He went about his business as usual, smoking his cigar. In the absence of the driver, he even dropped Tejimola to school. At lunch, he meticulously chewed his chicken salad thirty-two times with his thirty-two teeth. The household carried on as before even after Bohua's death, except for Tejimola's stepmother. Not long after the incident, she walked out of the house.

The night before her departure, the merchant had grabbed her by the hair. Seizing her long black tresses which, back then, used to go all the way down to her waist, he had given her a tight slap. She had sunk down on the marble floor, under the shade of the four-foot ornamental mango tree on the balcony. Her mistake had been asking Tejimola—who had come to sleep beside her father on the conjugal bed—to go to her own room. The merchant had grabbed his pillow and gone off to his daughter's room.

'Shakya Sourav cannot scratch her itch anymore, that's why the bloody whore is acting weirdly,' she had heard him hissing on his way out. Early next morning, she had returned to her own home.

She had ignored her mother's tears, her father's mutterings and the many accusations the merchant had made, linking her to Bohua. She stayed inside, refusing to leave her room to eat or wash. After two whole months, she went to the beauty parlour at the end of their lane and had her head shaved.

It was as if her action lent weight to the merchant's words. She faced every rumour without flinching—all the stories of how she had joined hands with Bohua, and hatched a plan to kill Tejimola and poison the merchant's food to claim his property. Her lover's death had driven her mad, they said.

It was a tale she began to believe herself. Around the same time, she finally confronted her uncle, driving him out of the door with a resounding slap. Strangely enough, the man hadn't been able to look her in the eye.

Why had it taken her eighteen years to slap him? The regret gnawed at her. Late at night, she rummaged in her cupboard and took out her brushes to paint a clear sky dotted with stars, around a bald-headed woman. There was no one else on the scene to taunt the woman. Distant rumours no longer singed her.

Despite all her ranting, her mother regularly massaged her head with sesame and jatropha oil. As a result, her hair grew back in fifteen days, leaving her head looking like a burflower, but she wasted no time shaving it clean with an electric trimmer. She didn't quite know whom she was mourning this way. Her husband, who hadn't allowed her to wear her sundress on their honeymoon in Goa? The cook, who had never let her make anything of her choice in her own kitchen? Her stepdaughter Tejimola, who had insisted on sleeping in the same bed as her father despite being twelve years old? Her uncle, who had bribed her with chocolates only to thrust his lollipop into her mouth? Bohua, who had promised her so much only to let go of her hand halfway?

All this took place three Augusts ago. Today, except for the title of Tejimola's stepmother, her time in the merchant's house felt like nothing more than a story. Society had moved on too, occupying itself with other tales, dragging down Tula's mother and the co-wives of Kite's daughter. Tejimola's stepmother's tale no longer trended on Facebook walls.

Tejimola's stepmother sported a pixie cut these days, but her hair had grown longer during the Covid lockdown. Long enough to be grabbed. She kept it tied in a short, stubby ponytail, just as her father had done for her when she was a child. It stopped the hair from disturbing her while painting, but her turmoil remained. It was torture to carry in her tresses an identity, a life she had long left behind. Most of the beauty parlours had been closed anyway. Unlike the parlour at the end of her lane, some of them had started re-opening now, but she knew not everyone could cut her hair the way she liked it. Today, after much enquiry, she finally decided to set out for the unisex salon in Six Mile.

Walking past the whining puppies and stepping out of the gate into the main road, Tejimola's stepmother was about to open her umbrella when she stopped, spotting a young girl in the distance.

Long, snake-like hair with split ends. Flaking skin. How thin she had grown! And yet, unlike her counterpart in the folktale, she didn't have trouble recognising her stepdaughter.

It was indeed Tejimola.

The grapevine had already brought her the news of the terrifying, despotic reign of the merchant's latest wife. It was good, she reflected, that the new wife was a strong-willed woman. Otherwise she too would have lost her name to the title of Tejimola's stepmother.

'Want a haircut?' she called out to the girl. Tejimola nodded. Yes, she did.

The girl spent the entire Uber ride violently scratching her head. Must be lice, thought Tejimola's stepmother. She would have to buy her a Mediker shampoo, and tell her to soak margosa leaves in water and rinse her hair with it.

Several lice dropped out of Tejimola's hair as the salon employees carried out the disinfection protocol at the entrance.

'Eww!' screamed the young woman who was spraying them with sanitiser, retreating hastily. She finished the thermal screening from as far away as possible.

Tejimola's stepmother stifled a laugh. Business must be slow because of the lockdown, or else a salon like this would have shooed Tejimola away from the doorstep.

A man appeared to ask if they would prefer tea or coffee with almond milk. A woman followed him. Her face above her mask seemed to be glowing. Tejimola's stepmother talked to her about a haircut. The woman informed her that the specialists would be occupied for three hours, and was telling her about all the treatments she could try for her acne-covered cheeks when her attention turned to Tejimola.

For the sake of decorum (read business), she held back the scream about to escape her lips and pitched a full hair and body rejuvenation treatment for Tejimola, and conveyed the costs of various options.

Tejimola's stepmother had gained weight during the lockdown. Regular honey with lemon juice and cups of green tea had proved useless, doing nothing to melt the fat which had accumulated around her breasts and bottom. With the central air-conditioning not working, the heat had begun to make her sweat. She started fanning herself with her hand, exclaiming how hot it was.

The woman jumped at the chance. Tejimola's stepmother

had become too flabby, she said, explaining why she was feeling so hot. The rake-like Tejimola would do well by gaining 2.49 kilos, while she herself would need to lose 3.20002 kilos in total, added the woman. Then they would both be just right to become calendar models. Their height, however, could still be a problem, the woman remarked. If only they had both been exactly 3.444449 centimetre taller.

'Even so, if you join our gym and lose some weight, I could try and make some arrangements,' she concluded.

Tejimola's stepmother had no particular desire to feature on a calendar. Nor did she want to burden her mind with such an elaborately negative assessment of her body. She stood up to leave, only for the woman to assume that she had convinced them with her unsolicited suggestions. She presented them with two forms.

'Madam, please fill these out,' she said. 'Write down your name and your daughter's, the father's name and other essential details, and wait a while on the sofa.'

Tejimola's stepmother smiled. She couldn't even remember the merchant's name anymore. Her eyes travelled to an advertisement on the opposite wall. She scanned the poster, beginning to laugh in her head at the sight of the man on it.

The merchant's face was glowing even brighter, thanks to the glossy paper, and possibly the fistfuls of almonds he must have consumed.

Who else but he could dictate how a woman's body should look, she thought to herself.

Long, beautiful hair. Blue-grey eyes. Teeth like pomegranate seeds, the colour of a drop of indigo mixed with half a litre of milk. A figure as curvy as an hourglass. A woman who didn't look like this was not fit to be a woman. She was wanton. Cursed. A witch. If this simple idea wasn't drilled into the heads of women like Tejimola's stepmother, the merchant's enterprise would bite the dust, wouldn't it? The beauty business ran the way the merchant wanted it to. Full breasts and heavy thighs—mistress. Those without these— calendar girl. And yet, it was the merchant who had his arm wrapped around the waists of both. Tejimola's mother began to roar with laughter, startling the woman who had until moments ago been pestering her with pointless advice.

She couldn't stop laughing all the way from VIP Road to Noonmati. Tejimola was surprised, but glad as well. Her stepmother's face lighting up with laughter had reminded her of her own mother. She had never laughed this way at home. Tejimola had kept her distance from her, and so had she. After all, people used to say all sorts of things. She had never had the opportunity to feel at ease.

Tejimola kept staring at her stepmother's face. The short-haired, shabbily dressed woman seemed to her at that moment like her mother. No, not quite that. A friend. A friend to whom she could pour her heart out.

Tejimola's stepmother stopped the Uber near an old hair-cutting saloon in front of the Noonmati Refinery. Sending away the surprised driver, she turned to Tejimola and asked once more, 'Still want a haircut? Or would you rather go home?'

The girl nodded again to say yes. She wanted a haircut. Whether she would go home or not was to be decided later.

Tejimola's stepmother grinned. The girl was finally acting

like her own offspring. They entered the saloon and asked the barber for a haircut. As they got their haircuts and head massages with B-grade Bollywood songs in the background, it finally dawned on her.

Panei had once been her name. Panei!

The memory, which she had thought was lost for ever, filled her with joy. Of course, she knew all memories, however dear, were memories best—one could peep at them, but never fully return. The title 'Tejimola's stepmother' was a cherished identity now.

After their haircuts, they went to a nearby Starbucks on the way back home. Sipping on her choco-chip-laced coffee, Tejimola's stepmother realised that her hair would no longer give her any trouble. She had finally found a place to get it cut.

A TOUCH OF A TREASURE

Jintu Gitartha

Translated by Harsita Hiya

He had thought he would never look back on the world he had left behind. Determined to do up his life according to his own wishes, he had made his home in a corner of the city. He had begun building his dream home brick by brick, just the way he had wanted to.

But do things always work out the way we want?

No.

No. At times, the colours escape the patterns in spite of our wishes, revealing impressions never seen before.

Perhaps the news of Sumi's wedding had in a way filled him with relief. It had given him an excuse to breathe freely, ignoring the easterlies which had made a mess of his otherwise mundane life. It was why he had resolved to attend it as soon as he had received his invitation.

Pushing his way through the crowd, he managed to find a seat for himself in the train to lower Assam, feeling as though he were stepping into another time. The train had already started moving at a sloth-like pace. He undid his ponytail, then made an Instagram reel and uploaded it to his Facebook stories, keeping a watch on his viewers. One of the first to view it was Antariksha Da—his hometown neighbour and former dance teacher.

Ah! He appeared to be in the grips of many emotions all at once.

He recalled a bewildering afternoon from the time he was flitting between boyhood and youth. Back then, he was a student of the newly built Jatiya Bidyalaya near his hometown of Tihu. The daily burden of school was so tiring for him that he tended to drift into sleep after lunch. On most days, his mother used to wake him up from his nap after she had changed the spot where the cattle were tethered. Although he was still drowsy, he would get to his feet and go off to practise his dance steps with Antar.

One two three four—round one!

Again! One two . . . Back, back. . .

One two. . .

But that afternoon was unusually quiet and still. He sat up in bed, awoken by a half-dream made even stranger by the sound of chirping crickets. In his dream he saw his body coming together in an unusual position with that of the tall, sinewy Antar, and discovered the erection of a natural truth.

He made several attempts to cut himself open thereafter on the dissection table of the laboratory called life, only to arrive at the same outcome every time.

The excitement he had felt on that mystifying afternoon of his boyhood helped him gather the courage to write those three magical words in Sumi's notebook during a water break at school.

'I love you.'

Before his newfound enthusiasm could die down, the school administration had decided to summon his parents.

He smiled now, remembering that moment. Today he had freed up his schedule for the entire day to attend the same girl's wedding.

Was the wedding truly the only reason he was going there? Or was it the desire to show off who he had become that was growing fiercer within him? By now his paintings had become renowned in art galleries across the world and achieved national honours. Several popular TV channels had broadcast interviews with him.

Again and again, he felt the urge to ask himself some questions.

But a cruel truth dug its raptor-like beak into his wound every time. He wanted to breathe freely, away from this suffocating life—to step out of the cave he dwelt in so he could bask in the heat of the sun.

He no longer remembered when exactly he had entered that cave. Perhaps when the cries of 'Leddis! Leddis!'—one of the taunts hurled his way for being 'effeminate'—became his constant companions. Or perhaps it was at another time, during the days he was unable to perform the difficult dance steps Antar taught him, and was forced to resort to the easiest classical moves inserted into modern songs. Not long after that, he gave up dancing for good. He had to, really. People like him who had spent their days dancing to old songs by Bhupen Hazarika and Zubeen Garg could hardly keep up with new trends like the 'cockroach'. He lost contact with Antar as well. He exhausted himself constantly for the longest time, trying to recover his interrupted dream. Then he poured this fatigue and sorrow into various colours and motifs.

He noticed that the darkness outside had taken on a strange hue. Cold air was sneaking in through the gaps of the closed window as the train moved ahead, lurching sideways every now and then.

The movement reminded him of how he had shuddered when his mother told him Antar had brought home a bride. That day had felt like a door slamming shut on him. Afterwards, he went on to hear about a court case. About the girl leaving her new home for good. He refused to pay heed to any such talk.

* * *

Shailen had arrived by then, sowing the seeds of a new dream in his life.

With him, he tried his best to recreate the half-dream of his youth, to bring to life that curious position in bed, only to feel disappointed after every instance. In the crevices of Shailen's body, he tried hunting for Antar's enchanting fragrance, the smell which had once so aroused him in those afternoons spent rehearsing new dance movements. His efforts were fruitless. An image of that precious position kept flashing before his eyes during every encounter.

Perhaps people come alive in childhood only to spend the rest of their days chasing dreams of the past.

He too had done this in the city, trying to find new ways to make sense of life. Amidst all this, he had met Shailen one day, a private-school art teacher whose painting was being displayed at an exhibition of the Artist's Guild at the time. The man, close to his age yet older, could barely speak coherently during their first conversation, his expression as awkward and hesitant as that of every junior artist who admired his art. He couldn't help but be attracted, feeling a longing to brighten Shailen's face with the flickering light of his own life.

He found himself standing in front of a group of bright faces. All his old classmates were sitting in a corner of the wedding venue, gossiping and whispering about his long hair, the snake-shaped ring on his finger and the trident stud in his ear. Some classmates working in private companies even came up to him to tell him how much they envied his artistic lifestyle.

He greeted everyone with smiles, his mind elsewhere. Returning to his old world after so many days had brought back memories in bits and pieces, summoning again the precious position from the half-dream of his childhood. Like the swelling froth of boiling milk, the budding feelings he had long ago developed for Antar began to rise in his chest once more. He wanted to open Facebook for a glimpse of Antar's profile, but Shailen's old messages popped up on the screen instead. He clenched his fist.

Everything in life has more than one door, doesn't it? Just like the Karbi myth he had once tried to recreate in a painting. He had first heard it on a visit to a Karbi Hills village.

'Don't go left. On the left is the road to hell.' An old Karbi woman had sung out to him, invoking the myth.

Later, at home, as he tried making a painting inspired by it, the colours and patterns came together to build an alternative door in front of him. Another way. It was as if the splattering paint wanted to revolt and ask him: Doesn't a door close only for a thousand others to reveal themselves?

It was the hope of such possibilities that paved the way for his conversation with Antar on Facebook. At the end, they agreed to go out together the following day.

He slipped away from the wedding venue before it got too late, anticipation taking hold of his thoughts.

* * *

The next afternoon carried the melody of gentle sun rays, the wind singing along with it. Antar cruised ahead in his Maruti 800. He had his own business now, a car-servicing outlet. The young crowd would come to him with special requests for modifications and graphics.

He stole glances at Antar's long, smooth neck. A new box back haircut had added to his uncommon looks. Antar's cologne gladdened his heart, just like the old days.

As Antar ran his fingers through his hair out of habit, a buried desire that lay coiled up like a snake in the depths of his memories came to the surface, baring its hood.

'What do you usually think about,' he asked, breaking the silence. 'I mean while driving?'

'I just keep my eyes on the road,' said Antar without looking at him. 'Music?' he added after a while.

'My choice!' he said with a grin.

'Go on then,' laughed Antar.

Billie Eilish's pained voice reverberated inside the car.

Retrace my lips

Erase your touch . . .

He looked outside as they drove down the highway, racing past barren paddy fields blighted by yellow.

Is this how we are supposed to race past those we once allowed into our hearts?

Shailen had once chosen a house for him in that exact shade of yellow.

He had just bagged an art scholarship from the Indian government at that time. With an ample allowance coming his way, he had decided to shift into a new home. Shailen had helped him look for one. As though he was certain life would forever go on the same way.

How could he? He thought to himself.

'I'm doing a bit of new work in music,' said Antar, lowering the volume.

'What kind of work?'

'Manike Mage Hithe, have you heard it?'

'The Sri Lankan song?'

'It's become a huge hit! So many remakes. I'm working on a Jhumur version.'

'Oh,' was all he could manage in answer.

He had always found it hard to care for anything wildly popular, preferring the work of Munch, and paintings like Kahlo's 'Without Hope' over Da Vinci's 'Mona Lisa' and Van Gogh's 'Starry Night'.

'What are you thinking?' asked Antar.

'Nothing, really. Haven't been down this road for a while.'

The car left the main road. It began gliding down a lane next to a deep-blue river that resembled a bright ribbon fluttering behind them.

* * *

The rain outside was relentless that night, accompanied by frequent lightning and thunder. Damp, cold air kept rushing in through the open window. It was the night Shailen had finally managed to break down the fortress of his will-power. They were lost in each other until dawn. The packet of condoms he had always taken such care to use remained in Shailen's bag.

Forgotten.

So many things remain forgotten.

Leaving the car in the resort's parking spot, Antar purchased two entry tickets. They sauntered across the huge lawn, the cool breeze from the river wrapping itself around them. Between rows of marigold flowers, they passed young couples sitting on bamboo benches, lost in conversation.

They settled down on one of the bamboo platforms built along the river bank. The sun seemed ready to plunge into the heart of the still, quiet river. As though, before parting, it wanted to embrace the slender frame tight enough to rattle its ribs.

'Tell me,' Antar whispered into the stillness.

'Wh-what?' he answered.

'What do you usually do at this hour?' Antar asked.

'Nothing,' he blurted out. 'Nothing important.'

What did he do? What did he do at this time? Often, he sat by the Sandhya–Lalita–Kanta, watching the sun try to bury its face in the hills. He recited the same old tale to the pebbles strewn around him. Wide-eyed, he stared at the stream hoping to find himself in the clear water, only to lose sight of his own reflection.

Was there anything more terrifying than being ashamed of oneself?

Perhaps we all sketch out our dream lover in our youth, merely trying afterwards to find them in people of flesh and blood. He too had done everything in his power to paint the Antar of his youth in reality, discarding every malformed and malnourished hue.

He glanced at Antar now, who was enjoying the heat of the sun as the wind ruffled his silky hair. He wanted so badly to hug him, but his memories carried him back to the GMC counselling room.

'Do you know the source?' The counsellor had asked. 'I mean from whom you—'

He remembered the phone call he had made to Shailen outside the Mahendra Mohan Choudhury Hospital, clutching the report. The sun was about to set in the city. The sky was the colour of a ripe mango steen. He could feel its bleak shade of red seeping into him bit by bit. Shailen had refused to get tested that day, despite all his pleading.

Those who remain in our memories are like thorns embedded in our skin.

All of a sudden, he sat up in shock. Somehow, he had found out I had been stalking him all this time; carefully looking for ways to do it—just for the sake of his story.

He rubbed his eyes and looked at me.

'Well, then. Have you any ending in mind? Anything befitting this tale?'

I lit a cigarette. Picking up my pen, I began to scribble—

'I often come across your posts on Facebook,' said Antar. 'Your work makes me so proud, truly! How great—'

'I am not that great, Antar,' he interrupted him, 'I am worse than you can ever imagine.'

'Good and bad—it's all relative, isn't it?'

'I used to have a boyfriend,' he said. A wild, earthy smell wafted in from somewhere. Antar inhaled deeply.

'And you . . . you used to be my crush.'

Drops of rain began to fall all of a sudden. They sought shelter in a nearby shed. Antar's old cologne filled his nostrils, making its way through his nerves to pierce his heart.

'Can you hear the rain!'

'These things are losing their charm for me,' replied Antar.

'Am I losing you too, then?'

'I don't know. Maybe I am the one who's lost.'

Darkness began to set in. Through the canvas of rain, they looked at the stars blinking over the other side of the forest. On that empty river bank, Antar took his hand between his palms. His hand, which had yearned so long to be touched, began to tremble and—

* * *

Out of the blue, he grabbed my wrist.

'Not every story has a happy ending,' he whispered.

He walked out, leaving behind a half-complete painting

in my room. I picked it up to study it. Underneath a night sky, on the indistinct outline of a palm, was the impression of a distinct position. The hand seemed poised to stretch out towards the left, in the direction of an invisible door in the darkness. I ran my fingers over the brush strokes.

'I call it "A Touch of a Treasure", writer sahab,' he said from the doorway. 'I'll be sending it off tomorrow for binding.'

ROOTS

Madhurima Barua

Translated by Syeda Shaheen Jeenat Suhailey

The village is named Ouguri—after the lake. Jayanti gazes at the huge lake from the shore. Someone is getting into a canoe to go fishing. The headman's six-fingered nephew perhaps, a lucky fellow, famous for how his net always snares the heaviest haul. Some say he waits by the lake, hunched in the shadows, accompanied by a fiendish water demon said to inhabit water bodies.

Turning her head, Jayanti sees her son Deepak sitting patiently with two fishing rods, waiting for the floaters to move. She is irritated. After passing his higher secondary examination, he had attended Soingaon College for a couple of years. But unable to clear the exams there, he now wastes his time fishing or wandering around the village. She also sees her eldest daughter Joya putting the fish caught in the bamboo traps back in the water, the jakoi and the khaloi, as she walks along the shore.

The sun is setting on the other side of the lake. A warm orange glow spreads over the area.

'I am back, Ma,' her youngest daughter Bijoya calls out from the back. Jayanti turns around. Bijoya is back from school.

'Wait, I'll be there soon. Change out of your uniform, your sister will give you something to eat.'

She walks back from the lake slowly, lays down a low wooden stool in the courtyard, takes the brass blade and starts sectioning areca nuts.

'Make me some tea,' she tells Joya.

Joya brings her a bowl of steaming tea and a couple of sweets on a plate.

'Good, now get down to studying before your father comes back. You cannot afford to fail the high school exams again.'

Joya lowers her head and walks back inside the house.

Jayanti regrets being so harsh with her daughter. The money her husband Champak makes as a daily labourer, and her own income from weaving and sewing, appear to have been wasted on Deepak and Joya, both of whom have failed the examinations this year.

Tring-tring. Suddenly, a cycle enters the courtyard, its bell ringing. The ramshackle cycle is louder than the bell.

Her thoughts are paused.

Startled, she returns to the present and turns towards the source of the sound—two laden bags are hanging from the handles, one with greens and vegetables, while the other has lentils and sugar. Her husband is entering the courtyard—a sight that makes her happier.

'Hold the cycle, Jayanti,' he says, trying to maintain his balance. She grabs the handle quickly, steadying the cycle so that he can dismount. A strong stench of country liquor assaults her.

The man is tottering.

Joya and Bijoya run out joyfully on hearing their father's voice, taking the bags off the handles. Jayanti pushes the cycle and props it up against the wall of the house.

'Oohkota!' she exclaimed in disgust. 'What a horrible smell! How can you drink so early?'

'Hey shut up, don't you speak, I drink vodka—I have vodka water. I—I drink vodka,' Champak boasts loudly in broken English, thumping his chest.

'Fine, fine, no need to shout so much. The neighbours will hear,' Jayanti tries to hush Champak in a low voice.

'You think I care even little? I work oil company—Digboi, Digboi—I speak English,' Champak screeches back in his pidgin English.

Whenever her husband comes into a bit of money, he drinks and makes a hullabaloo at home. It's not just her—her children find the situation unbearable too.

The use of hooch is spreading throughout Ouguri as well as neighbouring villages. The young men start drinking early, so much so that their internal machinery rusts by the time they are in their thirties. They end up with serious ailments that incapacitate them.

Jayanti looks at Champak, wondering why he started drinking—was it sadness? The sorrow of losing his job?

Alcohol and exertion had crushed and pulverised Champak. Sunken eyes, hollow cheeks, ribs protruding so prominently they could be counted, the torn shirt that hides nothing. The trousers he bought many years ago at the Soingaon haat are so worn out that it's a mystery how they stay on his waist. Her heart softens at the sight. He falls on the low stool instead of sitting on it—he's so drunk he's swaying like a bamboo reed caught in a gust of wind.

She leaves the man where he's sitting and goes into the kitchen. Joya is putting away the groceries. She spots the small liquor bottle that has rolled out of the pile of vegetables. The sight enrages her.

Snatching the bottle from Joya, she rushes to her husband and says, 'Don't you have any shame? All the swill you drunk wasn't enough, you had to bring more?'

'Stop your bellyache—I'm drinking with my own money, what business is it of yours? I have brought food for you as well. Pork liver and meat—cook it properly.'

As he continues grumbling, Champak vomits, then keels over and promptly passes out. She boils over in anger at the sight. This man is torturing her to death; the exaggerated lines on her face, indicating an age of much more than forty. Her body is already wrecked by gastric pain, she can endure no more. Going up to Champak, she pushes his body roughly, saying, 'Get up, get up, what have you done?'

He doesn't move. So what else can she do but fetch a pail of water from the well, pour it over his head, and then tug, pull and push his inert frame with Joya's help till they can lay him on the bed. She finds it difficult to carry his weight nowadays, a sharp pain shooting from her waist down to her feet, making her feel limp. She puts on the wraparound she bathes in, cleans the nauseating puddle of vomit and then pours two more buckets of water on herself near the well.

Daylight is fading; they need to light the lamps. Sitting on the verandah, Joya quickly cleans the soot-darkened glass-tops of the kerosene lanterns. Kerosene is expensive, and there is not much to spare—they use one on their study table and the other only when they have to. Jayanti makes use of an oil lamp in the kitchen.

Jayanti tells her two daughters, 'Get to your studies, I don't want to hear a peep out of either of you. Where is your brother? Is he still fishing?'

They say nothing, as they already know that their brother has gone out. Jayanti goes into her bedroom, puts on an old garment marked with smoke stains and enters the kitchen. She turns for a glimpse of their estate from the verandah.

About six years ago, they had cleared about five acres of land in the Soingaon Reserve by the Ouguri Lake. The vast area around them turns pitch dark as soon as evening falls. A handful of oil lamps twinkle in the distance, but the croaking of the frogs and the chirruping of the crickets make for an eerie atmosphere.

Jayanti pulls the bundle of dry branches, collected by the children from the jungle, closer to the makeshift stove and lights a fire. She puts the rice pot on it, chops the vegetables and prepares the spices and condiments for the meat. The fish Joya had caught earlier is already dressed.

There's a sudden sound outside, as though something has fallen over. She runs out into the courtyard where she sees the bicycle that she had propped up against the wall now lying on the floor. The nuts and bolts have come even looser. Jayanti picks it up and carries it inside. The bicycle is dear to her.

The sight of the damaged cycle on the floor brings back

an old image, as sharp as a jagged bolt of lightning. Jayanti used to cycle to school with her girlfriends at that time. One day she fell off the cycle on the way, and discovered that the rear wheel was all but flat.

Some men were working near the site for a rig that was to be built for the Digboi Oil Company. A tall, neatly turned out young man stepped forward from the group, picked up her cycle and asked, 'Are you hurt?'

An embarrassed Jayanti tugged her clothes from her knees all the way down to her feet, and shook her head. The man collected a pump from the digging site and re-inflated the tyre. Her friends had stopped and were waiting a short distance away. That was their first introduction—she came to know later his name was Champak Nath, and he was from Goalpara.

The memory of that incident brings a quick smile to Jayanti's face. She thinks of the shabby, scruffy, badly dressed man who used to be so handsome, warm and caring. Passing the bedroom on her way to the kitchen after putting the cycle away, she peeps at the sleeping Champak, who's curled up with his thin hands on his chest. A tender feeling touches her heart.

Jayanti suddenly remembers she has the rice on the fire—and rushes to the sputtering flames, feeding it some more sticks of wood. Gazing into flames, which are roaring again now, she is lost in her memories once more, wondering what she had ever seen in Champak. His attractive appearance and charming behaviour had lured in her adolescent heart, setting off colours as vibrant as the red poinciana.

Jayanti went through a period of quick growth after that

chance meeting—both physically and emotionally. It was just that she was the right age. They continued talking, in moments stolen between going to and from school. One day, he passed her a letter confessing his love for her. She trembled in fear and excitement, but her happiness was dashed when her father came to know of these conversations and made a huge fuss. 'I'm warning you,' he said, 'make sure I never hear of you talking to him, or else . . .'

Afraid of her father, she remained holed up in one corner of the house.

She knew that her family would never approve, that they would never agree to her marrying this stranger from Goalpara in West Assam. But the intensity of her feelings for Champak only rose.

The year had barely turned when they made their plans for the last day of her matriculation examinations. She filled her schoolbag with clothes, sought blessings from the deities at home and prayed for her parents' well-being.

She felt sad about the sister closest to her in age, but there was no time to look back. She got on her bicycle in a hurry, as if she were late for the exam. And when the exam was done, she eloped with Champak.

No one from her family went looking for Jayanti after this—perhaps her father had ordered that she be considered dead.

Champak painted a rainbow of all the seven colours on her eighteen-year-old heart. Clutching his hand, she started her new life wearing rose-tinted glasses. They lived in the town of Digboi for about eight months, but barely had she started living the life of her dreams, with no more than months having passed, a shocking incident took place, thoughts of which gives Jayanti goosepimples even today.

Jayanti's memory keeps working while her hands move mechanically. She takes the rice off the fire and puts on the pan for the meat.

That day too she was cooking their dinner. There was already a new life inside her body. Champak was late getting home from work. Suddenly, there were loud sounds at the door, and Champak rushed in, panic written all over his face, looking for all the world as though someone had whipped him.

'What's wrong?' a concerned Jayanti asked.

'I got caught, Jayanti. Ratan and the rest of them had asked me to go with them, but the guards caught us.'

'Caught whom?'

Wrapping his arms around her, he began to cry like a child, his voice betraying utter helplessness. Jayanti started shaking him, as though he had been struck by lightning.

'What's the matter, tell me everything.'

'Ratan and the rest of them have been stealing materials belong to the company and making money selling them outside. Ratan bought a motorcycle last month, and tonight they asked me to join them, because I wanted a motorcycle as well.'

'And then?' Jayanti shouted, her patience running thin.

'I made a big mistake in giving in to greed; I joined them.'

'You didn't even bother to tell me you've done something like this.' A scream tore through her breast, breaking her heart into bits. Her eyes were blurred with tears. She held

Champak close and broke down crying. That was the day the rainbow in her life changed its hues.

All of them were jailed. As expected, Champak lost his job. Even today, Jayanti trembles every time she recalls those distressing times.

With the doors of the oil company closed to Champak, a pall of darkness descended on them. It became impossible to look at Champak's eyes, the shadow of his crime eclipsed his face. After getting out of prison, he tried desperately to make a livelihood, but in vain. Then he went up to Jayanti and said to her, 'Are you asleep? There's something I'm considering.'

Being pregnant with their first child, she tired easily at the time. Lying on the bed with her eyes on the ceiling, she said, 'No, not yet. What are you thinking of?'

'You know the aged fitter at the oil company, Noren Kolita? He's inviting us to go and live in his village.'

'Doesn't Noren Kolita live here?'

'He's retiring next month, so he'll be going back to his village, Soingaon.'

'Soingaon? Where is Soingaon?' Jayanti had no geographical knowledge of this place.

'Soingaon, in the Kamrup district, beyond Guwahati.'

'Oh, that's a long way from here, isn't it?'

'Yes, pretty far, but there's no hope of another job unless this convicted criminal moves a long way from here.'

The world Jayanti knew stretched no further than Dibrugarh. Beyond that she had heard only of Guwahati— very far away, involving an entire day's travelling. They would have to go even further. How far was Soingaon exactly? She had no choice but to agree, for there was no other viable option. He had been too shamed to even leave his house after his release from prison. And she was assailed by a host of worries and anxieties, all of them jostling for space in her head. Champak seemed to have come up with the best option, and it was probably in her interest to agree.

'I don't know; do what you think is right, I don't feel very good about it.'

Happy to have obtained her consent, Champak said, 'Don't you worry now, we will go to Guwahati by train, you'll have no difficulty, and then around two hours more by bus.'

Jayanti wasn't up to worrying about anything. She had submitted herself to whatever time and fate would lead her to. The colourful poincianas began playing before her eyes.

Their savings amounted to a paltry sum of a few thousand rupees. For these new warriors in the battle of life, earning enough for themselves and managing two meals a day had become a grand dream.

Today, for some reason, sitting in front of the fire, Jayanti recollects her life at Soingaon. Champak shook off his jail-time-induced torpor and started working—as a day labourer. He even became a sharecropper for Noren Kolita. Deepak was born in the two-roomed hut that Noren Kolita built for them in his compound. How happy they had been that day! Joya came two years later. But she remembers that, when she had told Champak a few years later she was pregnant again, this time with Bijoya, far from being happy, he flew into a rage.

'What did you say? How will you feed another mouth?'

Gulping in fear, Jayanti nevertheless said, 'I'll manage, just the way I'm managing now.'

'What are you saying? Here I am, working till all hours of the night to pay for everything, do you understand any of this?'

How the man had changed, Jayanti reflected in dismay. Imagine so much hostility for a baby yet to be born.

'Joya,' she calls out. Usually, Joya helps her make dinner, but she has not shown up today. Then again, Jayanti does not like calling her children away from their studies.

Joya appears by the kitchen door on hearing her mother.

'Bring some more firewood,' Jayanti tells her, 'and then check whether your father has fallen off the bed.'

Joya goes out to the bundle of twigs they had collected and left to dry in the courtyard, gathers some of the sturdier branches and passes them to Jayanti before returning to her studies.

Jayanti shoves two of the sticks into the flames, her mind going back to the time spent in Soingaon by the bank of the Kolohi. Those were comparatively happier times for her. They made just about enough to cover daily needs, but it was peaceful.

Bijoya was born, and while initially Champak was not pleased, he grew to love and care for the young child. Some days after she was born, Champak said to Jayanti, 'I am thinking of buying some farm land in Monjora village, what do you think?'

Jayanti felt like jumping with joy. Masking her obvious happiness, she said, 'Do what you think is best. The community here is very good.'

'Yes, they have been so welcoming, they don't treat us like outsiders,' Champak agreed.

Jayanti started thinking about the home they would finally have in Monjora on the banks of the Kolohi.

But, man proposes and god disposes.

Five or six years later, in 2015, the year Deepak took his matriculation examinations, the rain began to sweep down. There was so much rain that it seemed as though millions of pitchers overhead were emptying themselves everywhere, for three or four consecutive days, swelling the river banks. The Kolohi was not particularly shallow, and its bed held abundant rocks and silt.

The government quarried sand from river beds like the Kolohi's, and Champak worked on these projects under the lessees, contractors and supervisors. The intensity of the rain that particular year made all the villagers who lived by the Kolohi fearful, the subject coming up constantly in their conversations.

'This will be it, the villages are going to drown, time to pack up whatever you can and get ready to leave if you want to save your life.'

Champak and Jayanti prepared too, packing their things and holding their children close. The night was dark, and rain unceasing. As parts of their dear village broke off and fell into the increasingly dangerous river, Jayanti felt her very flesh being torn off her body. The house they had built with their own hands, the garden they had filled with plants and trees were consumed by the raging river in front of their very eyes. Within moments they became destitute; a heart-breaking sight. Nature's relentless fury left them speechless.

The life they had made for themselves by the Kolohi was eroded with the same ease as the banks of the river. The cries and sighs of those who had lost their homes covered the embankment like a thick blanket. The Kolohi was cruel—just as she rested to provide fertile ground for agriculture, she also flooded her banks every year, turning the lives of many people upside down.

They felt blinded now that they had lost everything. Where would they go, what would they do? They stayed in government relief camps for some days, but it wasn't possible to live there for ever.

When they left the relief camp, Champak and Jayanti joined the ranks of the people befuddled by the loss of their homes, and entered the nearby reserve forest. Joining hands with neighbours from the Bodo and Rabha tribes, they began clearing the land together. They were aware that building a village here was illegal, but the need for survival was a stronger weapon than law and order in this battle.

The displaced people cleared enough land to build two villages. The enormous lake in the middle of the reserved area was called Ouguri in the east and Solsoli in the west. Jayanti and her family worked hard to clear their portion of the land, planted bamboo and banana trees and harvested rice and vegetables. The lake was filled with fish; many made a living by selling them at the Soigaon market.

The colours of Jayanti's life changed again. Champak had begun changing slowly—without a proper job, slaving to ensure two meals a day for his family and a perpetually hungry stomach made Champak seek out alcohol and he started drinking heavily. He drank country liquors like sulai and laupani, made by the local Bodos. After drinking, he would inevitably make a loud commotion. Jayanti worried that he would get drunk and fall into a ditch.

Today too he had come home with laden bags hanging from both sides of his cycle, which he could barely control, only by some miracle.

'Isn't dinner ready yet? Why is it taking such a long time?' Champak calls out from the bed. Jayanti shakes herself out of her reverie and blows on the flames to make them burn more strongly. The rice is done, the pork is simmering nicely.

'Joya!' she calls.

It is usually Joya's responsibility to clean the floor where they eat and lay out the plates and bowls as required. Jayanti suddenly remembers she has not heard her son in some time. Is he not home even at this late hour? Where is he, what is he doing? Her heart trembles.

She looks at Joya, who is leaning against the door in response to her mother's call. 'Isn't your brother home yet?' she asks.

'No,' answers Joya.

The veins in her forehead pulse with sudden worry. Where is he so late at night? 'Take the plates out, do you not hear your father shouting?'

Rising to her feet, she walks briskly towards the gate. There is deep darkness all around, but still she peers into it in all directions—and spots her son approaching in a stupor with slack jaws and an open mouth. She cannot yet identify the figure walking towards her, lit up dimly by a swarm of fireflies, but assumes it is Deepak. Spotting her, he asks in surprise, 'What are you doing here at this hour of the night?'

'Kotamora tu!' Jayanti says in exasperation. 'I came out looking for you. Where were you out so late?'

She leans forward to smell his breath—has he started drinking as well? If he has, she intends to give him a tight slap. But she doesn't smell alcohol and lets out a sigh of relief.

Jayanti feels better now that she knows her son has not been drinking. A gust of wind makes her shiver.

'Come in now,' she says in a softer tone.

Both of them move towards the kitchen.

They sit down on the floor in a circle for dinner by the light of the oil lamp. Jayanti starts serving everyone, looking at each of them in turn. Champak takes a few small bites of his food. Jayanti has not sat down to her meal yet, in case anyone wants a second helping. His mouth full of food, her son asks his father, 'Have you heard, Deuta?'

'Heard what?' Champak says with a sneer.

Her heart all but stops beating. What news has Deepak brought? She listens avidly. A bat flies past outside, flapping its wings.

'I heard at Tilleshwar Dai's house, they're going to avact us from the reservation,' her son says.

'Avact?' Champak asks with grudging curiosity.

'What is avact?' Jayanti repeats the question loudly. A chill runs down her spine.

'The government will clear out the villages in the reserve,' her son explains what he means by avact.

'Why? Where will we go? Why will they make us leave?' Jayanti's voice is full of dread.

Everyone's heart is running cold with fear.

'Why will they let us stay? This reserve is owned by the government. We built villages illegally,' Deepak says sombrely.

Champak sobers up at the conversation.

'We'll see who has the balls to throw us out. This is Champak Nath you're talking to.' He rises to his feet with bravado, done with his meal.

Deepak says, his eyes on his plate, 'Tilleshwar Dai said he will submit an application at the forest reserve office. Let's see.'

Joya's and Bijoya's eyes bulge with surprise—they forget to eat. Jayanti, who has just sat down to eat her own food, is in complete disbelief.

'You'd better eat, Ma, the lamp is about to go out,' says Joya. She begins clearing the empty plates, drawing them towards herself.

Jayanti keeps sitting in shock, beginning to feel dizzy. Every corner of the room seems to be shaking. She glances at the oil lamp, its flickering blackened tip giving off smoke—it is about to go out. She stares at the tip, her senses overwhelmed by a picture-perfect image of an azure sky over a blue, brimming Ouguri lake, lush green rice saplings swaying merrily in the wind on its shore, an image that disintegrates like the wisps of smoke running into her eyes, making them water. Her throat is dry, and she feels like she is floating where she has been sitting. She had begun to dream new dreams, would they wilt now?

The fantasy she had of a rejuvenated life with her family in Ouguri village is turning out to be a mirage. Just as a huge tree uprooted by a powerful storm crashes into the ground slowly, so too does Jayanti fall off her low stool in slow motion.

'Are you all right, Ma?' Joya and Bijoya rush to her and try to lift her off the floor. Deepak runs up as well.

Her vision fills with a series of images rushing past—all the people she has met in her life. Her half-remembered parents, the dream she had left her parents to follow, the house by the Kolohi, her home in Ouguri, all the dreams she has run after and never been able to catch.

When will the trial end?

Will her life end just like this? Where have the roots gone? She is engulfed by helplessness.

Clutching her children's hands, she tries to raise herself from the floor.

THE WATER SPIRIT

Imran Hossain
Translated by Mitali Goswami

And neatly folding the fishing net into halves and making two handfuls of it, Haren advanced to unfurl the net only to stop short in his tracks. Down the ribbony village alley, which seemed now to be floating in a mass of fog, he was coming that way. A peculiar manner of walking and his crooked and grotesque posture made it easy to recognise him even from a distance. In the flickering moonlight that came filtering down the slender leaves of the thin bamboo grove, his dew-wet ugly body shone with an eerie brightness. His human form seemed imbued with a strange ghostliness.

The gathering fog lingering over the water, the hustling sound of the wind blowing across the bamboo grove and the hazy, stripped moonlight all combined to give the shores of the lake a magical hue. Quite fearsome even in daylight now in the foggy moonlight, the place seemed even more haunted and mysterious. Now, the familiar paths, trees and shrubs and the boats of various sizes kept upside down on the bank of the lake, all seemed strange and unfamiliar.

The river was not a great distance away; in fact, a part of the lake even flowed into the Kolong. Yet, for the surrounding Kaiberta, Kalita and Lalung villages this lake was the lifeline. Their simple lives centred on this lake. The whole day long, the western side of the lake resounded with the cheery voices of the village maidens and youths, as they bathed or fetched water or swam on the lake surface. Moreover, the village fishermen with their big or small boats were to be seen unfurling their big or small nets almost all over the lake during the day. But everybody feared this north-eastern side of the lake, especially the edge of the cremation ground where aged giant elephant apple or Ow tree stood menacingly spreading its numerous branches. Even the Sylheti fishermen who worked for the fish merchants gathered up their nets and did not venture out in that direction.

The elders of the village say the place is haunted. It was here that, coming to fish on a bright full moon night, Ratneswar Bora had seen floating on the lake surface a boat of gold. Frightened out of his wits, he managed somehow to reach home and was at the bamboo bars of his gateway when he lost consciousness. When he came to, his body was burning with fever. He started strange mutterings about a boat of gold with oars of silver, of treasure buried under the Ow tree and so on. People say that Ratneswar would not have survived that ordeal had not his older brother Suren gone to Rajamayang that very day to get charmed oil from a renowned faith healer. Ratneswar, then a strapping youth, was an old man now, his hair and beard grown grey and his face lined with wrinkles, yet he never tired of recounting his experience as vividly as if it had occurred only the other day. For, many years after that, people, out of fear, had avoided going to that area until it took on an abandoned and deserted look. But, unable to fulfill the needs of his newly wedded wife with the proceeds that he gathered from petty thefts, Hebang had once tried to dig beneath the Ow tree. No pot of treasure was unearthed; only it is said that he did find a few gold coins. But he did not live to enjoy them. That very night he began to vomit blood and died, leaving his new bride in a widow's garbs.

But, for the people of the lakeside, the most astounding occurrence was that of the water spirit killing Tikheroo, transforming himself into Tikheroo's shape and then coming to live with Padumi, Tikheroo's young and beautiful wife. Till today, the spirit would have been slave to Haren Mahalder, and would have guarded the lake for him, had he not escaped after tricking Tikheroo's mother into giving him back his magical pouch which had been kept safe within a casket full of mustard seeds.

Back in those days, when the spirit was slave to Haren, the Mahalder's house overflowed with cash and kind. But Haren's luck seemed to have fled along with the spirit. His state deteriorated and he took to smoking opium, drinking and gambling the whole day, which took a great toll on his health and money. So much so that Haren, who used to provide fish for the entire village on festival days from his own lake, now took to fishing furtively on the lakes of others.

'Bak' the spirit is gone; seven years have gone by since beautiful Padumi's death. But their son Goroi remains. The village folks say that he too is a Bak spirit, being the son of the Bak. Otherwise, why would he incessantly roam along the side of the lake day in and day out?

For the past six or seven years, Haren has lived on what little he earned by fishing secretly on this north-eastern part of the lake. Here he could fish undisturbed except for a few stray jackals. But, for the past year, Goroi's mysterious presence in this area has caused him a lot of trouble. On the dark moonless nights of the dark phase of the moon, the krishnapakshya, Haren avoided coming to this part of the lake and unfurled his net somewhere in the vicinity of the village itself. But on bright moonlit nights of the suklapakshya, fearing that he would be caught poaching by the keepers of the Morigonya Mahalder's lake, he ventured out by the lonely, deserted stretch by the Ow tree. Just before dawn, keeping his net hidden by some bushes, he hurried home down the narrow alley. But now, fearing a meeting with Goroi on the way home, he took a roundabout way through the undergrowth of small bushes and shrubs. Frequently, Goroi would come this way with the steady, heavy stride of one walking in sleep. He would stand by the Ow tree, staring down at the glittering waters of the lake. Haren mused about it but could not understand why Goroi should behave so. Haren was his nearest neighbour; the lad had literally grown up in his backyard. Yet Haren hadn't a clue as to why the boy was behaving so strangely these days. Goroi's behaviour had given rise to many a rumour in the village. Each one had something different to say. Nitai, the fisherman from

Sylhet and Mayarani, Paran's mother, whispered: Call of the darkness, call of the spirit, he is allured by the water spirit. Some days ago, an LMP doctor from a nearby tea estate had come to visit the village head. He brought up the subject of sleepwalkers and disclosed that certain people were prone to walking in their sleep without knowing that they were doing so. The villagers, of course, saw no truth in such unseeming things. Whosoever believed in a man walking in his sleep would also believe in hair sprouting on a frog's back. They knew otherwise. They knew that the water spirit called Goroi to the lakeside on moonlit nights. Sitting beside the Ow tree, father and son would devour raw fish throughout the night and, when day dawned, the spirit sent his son back home. Some of them had even seen Goroi following the spirit to the lakeside. Amongst them, Heremba had given such a vivid description of father and son that most villagers had stopped going outdoors at night even to answer the call of nature. On the last Ekadasi, Heremba was in the opium joint from where he came out to urinate and saw Goroi walking behind a tall shadowy figure towards the lake. He even recalled seeing Goroi holding on to the fishing net hanging from the shoulder of the mysterious figure. Gravely, the village folk remarked, why shouldn't he? He was the water spirit's son after all.

No matter whosoever said so, old Pabhoi, Goroi's grandmother, refused to believe in such wild tales; deaf as she was, if she came to know of anyone speaking of such things, she rebuked them, soundly cursing them to her heart's content. She would cry out loud for all to hear, 'Goroi is my grandson. My Tikheroo's son. Which whore's son says that he is the spirit's offspring. Bring him to me and see if I do not beat him black and blue with my mekhela. May the gourds of such an evil speaker's garden turn bitter . . . may his face fester with sores, the bastard.' As a matter of fact, old Pabhoi could hardly bring herself to believe that her son Tikheroo was no more, that he had not returned after that fateful fishing expedition. How was she to believe it? Didn't she know that, in all the villages surrounding that lake, her Tikheroo was the best swimmer in all Morigaon? None but he dared to swim across the entire length of the lake at one go. Why, did he not remain underwater for the whole day fixing a trap of bushes and shrubs to entrap the fish? The lake was his second home, why would any spirit of the lake want to kill him? Those who had seen him even once could not erase his memory from their minds. He was amazingly adept at catching fish. Not only the small puthi khalihana, but also the large rohu and barali fish seemed to just flow into his net. At the time of Magh-Bihu when the whole village descended on the lake with their fishing nets and tools, it was always Tikheroo who made away with the biggest catch. On other days, Tikheroo used to sell his fish either at the Hindu village nearby or at the village market, but on such festive days he always distributed his catch among the villagers. But the villagers could not enjoy his generosity for long. Soon the government levied a tax on the lake so loved by the villagers and they came to know that the lake was to be auctioned off. On coming to know of the auction, the people of the village raised a hue and cry. But all in vain, as the richer section of the villagers, themselves hoping to become Mahalders, turned deaf ears to the entreaties of the village folk. And, one day, the lake was indeed auctioned off. To everyone's surprise, Tikheroo's cousin Haren, who passed his days in fights and quarrelling and nights in opium smoking became, almost overnight, the new Mahalder of the lake.

Of course, he did not become the sole owner; with him were two other fish merchants from Morigaon who became co-owners of the large lake. But Haren was the most fortunate among them for he got the best portion of the lake to himself. He got the most productive north-eastern part, starting from their village and ending by the Ow tree near the cremation grounds of the village. From the very next day, Haren stopped the villagers from fishing in the lake. Defying his orders, a few villagers did venture out to the lake but Haren, flaring up like an angry water snake, rushed out at them. Soon a great furore erupted and the quarrel would have got out of hand had the village head not explained the government rules and regulations to the simple villagers. About three days after that, the quiet lake surface was invaded by fishermen from Sylhet and Bihar. Among them the villagers were surprised to see Tikheroo also. He stood out in their midst, tall and dark as a sol fish.

Tikheroo's presence among the strangers came as a surprise to the villagers. All knew of the feud between the families of Haren and Tikheroo. The two families, though closely related, were not even on talking terms. Even if her family had to go hungry for days, Pabhoi never stepped towards Haren's house. Things had been much better when her husband Betharam was alive. But, unfortunately, early in life, he contracted tuberculosis, and the disease killed him. Upon his death, his younger brother Paniram, Haren's father, seizing all, drove poor, widowed Pabhoi with her infant son, Tikheroo, out of their home. Everyone in the village knew of the great hardships Pabhoi had to face in order to bring up her son, Tikheroo.

Anyway, the villagers were rather pleased to see their own Tikheroo in the lake among the unfamiliar fishermen. But gradually he became an object of envy for the other fishermen whose entry was banned on the lake, and whose only source of livelihood was thus taken away from them. Their once-loved Tikheroo became like an underwater thorn for them. The fact that he was Haren's kin now surfaced in their minds as a dead body surfaces in water.

Actually, it was not for any feelings of kinship that Haren had engaged Tikheroo. Opium-fuddled as his mind was, nonetheless he was aware of Tikheroo's great dexterity in fishing. He knew full well that someone like Tikheroo would be an asset to him in the business. So, the night before formally starting to fish in the lake, Haren came to his aunt Pabhoi and fell at her feet, imploring her to forget old feuds. The elders of the family were now no more. What good would it do to remember old quarrels, he reasoned. His wife was a sickly woman, he said, and entreated his aunt to return home once again to take up the reins of the house in her able hands. Such requests could not move old Pabhoi but when Haren, whom she had brought up, whom she had carried piggy-back many a times, started weeping a sea of tears, old Pabhoi found herself unable to resist any longer. That very night, along with Haren, Tikheroo and his mother made their way back to their ancestral home and began to stay in the same compound.

The next day, fishing was formally begun on the lake by Haren's men, after holding a pooja to appease and worship the lake god. At the crack of dawn, a huge barali fish caught on Tikheroo's net was chosen and its forehead dotted with vermillion. The fish was then released back into the water. A few fishermen made offerings of milk and salt while those from Sylhet arranged their own Pooja of Gangadevi. From that day, fishing began in earnest on the lake. Tikheroo not only competed with the Bihari and Sylheti fishermen to catch more fish but also taught them many new tricks of the trade. The more expert of these fishermen were a little condescending at first, but after a week or so they too acknowledged his sheer mastery. Initially, Haren found it a little difficult to understand this new business, but due to the honesty and skill on Tikheroo's part, he still made better profit than his partners. Hoping to make even more profit without putting in any effort of his own, Haren not only allowed Tikheroo to put up a house for himself in his own backyard but also handed over the running of the business to him, putting him in charge of the fishermen as well as the lake.

By the turn of the year Haren was able to buy many a plot of land in and around the village. Soon his stores overflowed with rice and his fishing business spread to Morigaon, Jagiroad and as far as Guwahati. The newly rich Haren changed a lot in manners and dress. He now began to wear a proper long dhoti and kurta like the clerks of the nearby tea gardens. To avoid the company of his old cronies and fishermen friends, he stopped frequenting the opium den. His very look changed and so did his manners as he put on airs as if he was the great merchant Bhola Saud himself. On the other hand, Tikheroo's health deteriorated due to his excessive labour. He spent most of the day under water and, perhaps due to this, became a little hard of hearing, his cough too began to trouble him all the time. Yet his zest for work did not lessen. Even when ill, he would fish from dawn to dusk tirelessly. Near the lake was a Tongighar, a small bamboo hut on stilts, used by the Mahalder's men to guard the lake at night. It was here that Tikheroo loved to spend most nights, with the fish spread out around him even after the rest of the fishermen had gone back to their villages for the night.

Many a times, on an empty stomach, Tikheroo would lie awake far into the night, the stench of raw fish around him, till dawn. The very little time that he stayed at home, he remained silent and unobtrusive. Most of his time at home was spent in the open space behind his hut mending and repairing old nets owned by the Mahalder or in weaving a new one. His being or not being at home made little difference to his mother, now weakened by age and severe ailments. Pabhoi had her hands full with running her own house and pitching in to help at Haren's whenever his sickly wife found it too much to manage. She had long given up the hope of any daughter-in-law of her own coming to aid her in her old age and gave all her tenderness to Haren's wife. Tikheroo was now almost two score years of age. No amount of coaxing or cajoling could make him agree to a marriage. Pabhoi had almost given up on the idea. But one day, to the immense surprise of the villagers, Tikheroo arrived home with a young bride in tow, a girl from Mayang, as comely as a mermaid.

About four years before, Haren's wife Seuti, too, had given birth to a son. But it was a tadpole-like, premature, still-born child, and she had showed no sign of motherhood after that. They had consulted renowned faith-healers but to no avail. Haren's infertile wife became even sicklier as the days passed. Despite his immense wealth, Haren remained constantly disturbed by the fact that he was childless. During the day he busied himself with his business but at night, when his raggedly and wretched wife settled down to sleep beside him, he found himself extremely disturbed, as his nagging worries seemed to return and their bed seemed to droop under the weight of their sighs. That was why Haren had send Tikheroo to Mayang in search of a cure. Tikheroo, who was to return a day after, came back after spending three days in Mayang. The old faith-healer sent a cure of potherbs mixed with the flesh and blood of the rhino for Haren. Along with the cure he also sent his beautiful young daughter as bride for Tikheroo. That evening, when Tikheroo's young bride alighted softly from the covered bullock cart, the whole place seemed to fill with the fragrance of turmeric and black pulses and that of the lotus used for the ritual wedding bath of the bride.

After evading the subject of marriage for so long, the sight of Padumi must have made him readily agree to marry. But how long did he enjoy the bliss of his married life? Barely two years after his marriage, Tikheroo left home one night for fishing and never returned. Padumi saw him for the last time that day, in the evening, as she lighted the lamp near the Tulsi plant in their front yard. In the fading evening light, she saw her husband standing in front of their store room talking to his mother. Even in that dim light she could make out that he was dripping wet. The net that hung from his shoulders was wet and water was soaking down his clothes. As she glanced at him, some strange foreboding seemed to cross her mind. That evening, even without bidding goodbye to Padumi, Tikheroo left for fishing.

When there was no sight of Tikheroo even three days after that, a worried Pabhoi informed the villagers, who gathered at their courtyard, of his disappearance. As the crowds increased, Padumi drifted in and out of consciousness several times. Their house and courtyard filled with people and it was then that Haren with utmost reluctance revealed the truth. What he had to disclose seemed like some fairytale to them. Some nightmarish, fantastic, unbelievable tale. He said that, some six months back, on hearing the sound of fishing near the Ow tree, he and Tikheroo had made their way there. On reaching the place, they found no one and, hence, gathering courage, they proceeded right on to the cremation ground. Again, finding no one at the spot, Tikheroo had decided to do some fishing on his own. His net was in the boat. Chanting certain hymns, he unfurled it and in no time had a good catch. After some time, feeling an urge to urinate, he paddled the boat towards the bank. Returning a little later, he settled down at one end of the boat. Thinking that Tikheroo must be tired after his bout of fishing, Haren himself began to row the boat. After crossing the Ow tree, Haren noticed a decrease in the amount of fish in the boat. At that instant, he also heard the sound of someone swallowing. Slightly turning his face, he saw clearly by the light of the moon that Tikheroo was devouring the fish raw. Haren at once understood what must have happened. Having strangled and killed Tikheroo and taking his shape, the spirit was now on the boat, a spitting image of Tikheroo himself. Seeing that the spirit was busy eating, Haren hurriedly rowed ashore and quickly grabbing the magic pouch of the spirit, made his way to the granary in their house. Immediately throwing the pouch into the big casket full of mustard seeds, Haren began to tremble with fear when he heard the sound of someone crying outside. Peeping out through the slits in the bamboo wall, he saw the water spirit weeping piteously, asking that his pouch be returned to him, he was powerless without it. Haren did not return the pouch. So the water spirit, unable to change back to his own form, remained as Tikheroo in their house for the last six months. Haren too remained silent, not knowing how to reveal the truth to the young bride Padumi. On the previous evening, saying that Haren wanted the pouch, the spirit got Pabhoi to get it for him from within the mustard and thus had the chance to run away, taking the magical pouch with him.

On hearing Haren's tale, old Pabhoi broke down in heartrending cries, mourning for her son. Padumi's wails swam in the air like the sad floating notes of a flute. The villagers, on hearing them, joined in. The very air seemed stilled by Padumi's anguished cries. Her sobs seemed to move the waves of the lake to turbulence. The cries and moans of the villagers seemed to be echoed by the clouds themselves until the sounds of mourning blended with the sound of the terrible storm and heavy downpour which came soon after.

Amidst the crowd of mourners in the house and the sound of the storm outside, no one took notice when Padumi slipped out and ran like one crazed in the direction of the lake. As the sound of the storm subsided along with the sound of the mourning, old Pabhoi noticed Padumi's absence and started running towards the lake. Not knowing what the matter was, the villagers too followed her and came to the bank. Here they saw Padumi sitting on the bank, gazing down at the water like one in a trance. Thousands of dead fish were afloat in the water.

From that day onwards, luck seemed to forsake Haren as his fishermen hauled up netfuls of dead fish and snail shells day after day. Thinking that someone had cast an evil eye on the lake, Haren sent for a quack from Pabakathi. But the quack, who descended to the lake with provisions of food and water and his hubble-bubble, could not unearth anything even after three days of mumbo-jumbo in the depths of the lake.

Seven months later, after a night of excruciating labour, Padumi gave birth to a boy-child. Purple hued like a water hyacinth, the baby was an ugly one. That night too, a storm raged overhead, followed by rain. In that rain, fish had fallen, not dead but alive, hoards of fish, Goroi fish in great abundance rained down from the sky. On the day of his birth, since their courtyard was covered with a large number of Goroi fish, people took to calling the baby Goroi.

Of course, Padumi had chosen a nice name for her son and used that name only. She had named him after some flower. Like Padumi, Haren's wife Seuti too called him only by his proper name. Unlike the others, Seuti was never repulsed by his ugliness. She extended her skinny fingers towards the baby and gently stroked the throbbing chest of the child. But neither Padumi nor Seuti lived long to call him by his actual name. Within a year of his birth, Seuti grew even more emaciated and passed away. Padumi, on the other hand, bloated to an immense size and died, leaving her three-year-old son behind to be cared for by Pabhoi. Anyone seeing her at the time of her death would hardly believe that she was once so narrow of waist, so slim and pretty. It is said that back in Mayang her father had some old enmity with another faith-healer and this man took his revenge by making Padumi swell up like a pot.

Padumi died a painful death due to her illness, but, till the time of her death, as long as she could, she continued to look after her son and mother-in-law, and do the rest of the household chores. But Pabhoi could not accept the fact of her daughter-in-law cohabiting with the water spirit. Moreover, how could she accept the spirit's son as her own flesh and blood. At the beginning, she had tried to coax Padumi into aborting the child but Padumi had been adamant. Secretly, she had mixed potherbs in Padumi's food to get the child aborted but in spite of all this Goroi was born. Though Pabhoi did not enter the room to assist her, Padumi gave birth to her son. Pabhoi never took the child on her lap but the child survived and was soon running about not needing to be carried about at all. Yet, at the age of three when he was orphaned, old Pabhoi's stone-like heart melted with grief. To the surprise of the large crowd at her doorstep, she gathered the child to her breast wailing, 'Do not cry my grandson, I, your grandmother, am yet alive.' Under her tending, gradually, Goroi's purplish-black complexion began to lighten until it almost resembled her wheatish one.

As a child, Goroi too, like the others of his age, spent his time flying kites or searching for wild cats among the tall grass of the surrounding fields. His large eyes, rough skin and hunched back did not deter the other children from playing with him. Then they neither feared nor hated him. His funny stature, in fact, made him all the more attractive to them. They felt drawn to him because of his funny posture, lisping words and his innocent smile. He was never angry if anyone called him the spirit's son. Instead, he would clap his hands and laugh aloud strangely, making a peculiar hiccup-like sound. Whenever he was happy, he laughed like that.

Though unnatural in looks, in manners he was completely natural. As he grew in age, he came to realise the import of many things. As he herded the village head's cows along with the other men, he came to know and understand much. Now he fully understood the true meaning of many a comment made by the villagers in passing. Now when the youngsters pointed to him shouting out, 'The spirit's son! The water spirit's son!', instead of laughing at them, he began to throw stones in their direction. Day by day, he grew more morose and angry. His friends too did not escape his anger. Even simple jokes provoked him and he lunged at them stick in hand. Now the only person who could still claim some intimacy with him was the village headman's son Dhaniram.

Though Goroi was a menial, Dhaniram affectionately called him 'friend'. Goroi too meticulously carried out whatever was asked of him by Dhaniram. Every morning, after leading out the cows to graze, Goroi came to Dhaniram and spent most part of the day with him. He remained with Dhaniram, like a shadow, all day long. Dhaniram himself was quite fond of the boy. But one day he too passed a demeaning comment about Goroi's birth. Many indirect comments had reached Goroi's ears but till then none had dared to speak so directly to him on this matter. And it was thus that the truth dawned on him. This time without retorting or getting angry Goroi kept staring at Dhaniram, a mute and hurt look in his eyes. For a long time, he remained sitting like one thunderstruck. Suddenly, like a pebble released from a sling, swiftly, he ran home without a word to anyone.

That night, it was only after a lot of cajoling that old Pabhoi could persuade Goroi to come into the kitchen for his meal. She lovingly served him his favourite curry of sol fish cooked in radish and smoked fish with a pinch of salt and mustard oil. Noticing that even the aroma of his favourite dish aroused no enthusiasm in him she remarked, 'These are all man-made stories boy, all wild tales. These simple villagers may believe in such concoctions but I don't. No matter what people may say, I know you are my grandson, my Tikheroo's son. Your mother Padumi was as comely as a mermaid. From far off Rajamayang, your father had brought your mother as bride. Would you like to hear it? Have your meal first then I shall tell you of their marriage. 'As comely as a mermaid was your mother,'— this oft-heard line gave a strange pleasure to Goroi. Several times, on other occasions, Goroi had heard of his mother's exquisite beauty. Sometimes, peering at his own ugly reflection on the still waters of the lake, he tried to recollect his mother's face. Somehow, he could never fully reconstruct that long-forgotten face. Only like some haunting melody heard from afar, like the fading notes of a lullaby sung by a mother to her child, hazy and indistinct, the figure of a faceless woman formed in his mind's eye. Yet he did have distinct recollection of one event from his early childhood. One day, when his mother was washing clothes and had left him to play by the lakeside, engrossed in his play he slipped and fell right into the lake. Sick as she was, Padumi too jumped into the lake and it was quite a while before she found him and swam ashore with him safe in her arms. People said that the water spirit had taken back his son. It was only because the mother went to ask for the child that the spirit returned it. Goroi's short life had almost come to an end that time. Fearing a recurrence, Padumi made an offering of his navel cord preserved since his birth, a few matchsticks and an egg to the lake, praying for long life for her son. He never learnt to swim like the other boys of his age. That incident had instilled a deep fear of the water in his mind and he never attempted to learn.

That night, holding Goroi in the circle of her arms, close to her breast, old Pabhoi began to speak of her son Tikheroo. Like a small boat left adrift, Goroi floated in the waves of old Pabhoi's tale. Till late into the night, Pabhoi continued her story until, unknowingly, she drifted off to sleep. But Goroi lay awake. With eyes wide open, he peered into his grandmother's face, trying to trace in that face the face of his father.

A long time after that, the moonlight crept in stealthily, perhaps right into the recesses of old Pabhoi's mind. Her thin angular body, now curved in sleep, straightened a little. The air in her throat blending with the saliva in her mouth came out like a tortured groan and, suddenly in her sleep, like a gushing water spout, words gushed out of her mouth . . . 'How many times had I forbidden her to go to the lakeside all by herself? With beauty like hers something was bound to go wrong. Did she listen to me then? Did she? Ashamed, she felt shy to bathe together with the other women of the village. She had to go alone. My worst fears came true . . . the water spirit was enamoured by her looks. He killed my son to live with her. He too ran away, taking the magic pouch with him. What do I do with this boy now? Whatever do I do with him?'

What she muttered now was a total reverse of all the tales she had told him in her waking hours. With a sinking heart, he heard his grandmother too reiterate the fact that he was indeed the water spirit's son. No wonder the women of the village mocked him and the children, pointing their fingers at him, shouted 'the spirit's son, the Bak's son'. He was truly the spirit's son, but then where was his father? Where did he live? Was it in the depths of the lake or in the marshes near the cremation ground? Where?

Leaving his bed, Goroi had then gone looking for his father; right up to the lakeside. Wandering to and fro, he grew tired and stood by the Ow tree. There, sitting in the dark, a few yards away, was Haren. With his net unfurled, Haren sat, drifting in and out of sleep. The sight of Goroi at the foot of the Ow tree sent a chill of fear through Haren.

He was, by nature, a fearless man but now he felt a strange fear. He did not believe in any ghost or spirit but today the sight of Goroi in the light of the moon made his heart beat faster. He, in fact, thought the shady figure to be that of some spirit. From that time onwards, Haren frequently spied Goroi, wandering restlessly by the lakeside on moonlit nights when he came this way to fish. He did not know whether Goroi came this way on dark, moonless nights too.

Apprehending that Goroi would disturb his fishing, Haren came to the lakeside a little early. But the net on his shoulders did not touch the water that night. As Haren glanced at the bright full moon reflected on the lake water, he was suddenly reminded of Padumi. Indeed her beauty had been like that of the full moon, bright and ethereal. Like a sweet fragrance floating in from a distance, the memory of a day, eleven years back, came to Haren's mind.

That day, Tikheroo was away from home and so Haren himself had to spend the night guarding the fish in the tongi-ghar. At the crack of dawn, he sent out fish to Morigaon and Jagiroad and started on his way home. Taking a short cut instead of the road, he was advancing down the lakeside and had not yet reached the bathing place of the village maidens when a sudden sound in the water attracted his attention. Peering down into the water, he saw Padumi swimming with strong back strokes, her face up towards the sky. Through her wet clinging clothes, her dark-hued body was clearly visible. She had been married for almost a year now. Right behind Haren's house was their small hut. Yet, in the course of that year, Haren had seen her at close range only once and on that day he had jokingly remarked to his sister-in-

law, 'What charmed betel nut have you fed my brother?'
He remembered that, instead of retorting, Padumi had
blushed red, veiling her face even further. A bashful girl,
she always ran indoors at the sight of Haren after that. The
name Padumi always conjured up the image of a pure and
innocent face to Haren. But that day the sight of her in the
water made Haren stop in his tracks. Among the lotuses of
the lake, she too seemed like a lotus as she floated leisurely.
But soon, turning in the water like a fish, she took a deep dive
to the depths of the lake, emerging a long time after at the
side of the lake among the small waves. Once again, breast
upwards, she floated. The soft morning light made visible
her conch-like breast, the deep whirlpool of her navel and
her creel-like narrow waist. And playing in and out of the
wave like contours of her smooth slippery body was to be
seen hundreds of tiny fish. For a long time, Padumi remained
in the water. Using her legs like a mermaid's fins, Padumi
swam in the water almost setting it afire with the unearthly
glow of her beauty. That day, the lake water was not the only
thing set afire. The same fire was in Haren too. Jealousy and
passion raged in Haren. After burning in that heat for quite
some time, on a rain-drenched night, he satiated his passion.
Asking Tikheroo to remain in the tongi-ghar, Haren entered
the ramshackle hut where Padumi slept like one dead. Haren
lay down by her side. At the time a fragrance like that of the
lotus seemed to be wafting out of her, body. In that heady
fragrance, he invaded her body, slithering in like an eel.
Outside, the monsoon raged incessantly and the fish of the
lake moved upstream in shoals.

Tired out by her day's work, Padumi slept soundly. She

was used to Tikheroo coming in late at night, sometimes even after midnight. That night too, taking Haren to be her husband, she lay unsuspectingly, drowsy, half-asleep and would have drifted back into the river of deep sleep had she not become conscious of a strange hardness and unfamiliarity of touch. In her sleep-benumbed state too she was conscious of a weight upon her breast and tried desperately to push it off but failed. A dark strong hand came down on Padumi's open mouth before she could scream. The bolting rain outside flooded the lake, drowning her groans.

Padumi was innocent. Despite all that had happened, she was innocent. In spite of everything, the thought that someone other than her husband had touched her did not arise in her mind even once. Thinking that it was some evil spirit, she got up, took a bit of mustard oil and invoked a charm to ward off the evil eye. Once again, she lay down but sleep evaded her for a long time and it was only early in the morning that she drifted into an uneasy slumber. Her sleep was disturbed by strange dreams. She dreamt that Tikheroo's body had bloated up like that of a pregnant woman and someone was whispering that he was expecting a son. That was not the only time. On another night too, smearing himself with raw fish, Haren came to Padumi's hut to drown once again in the lotus-like fragrance of her body.

As these thoughts came to Haren's mind, even in the freezing cold, Haren grew warm. A slow smile flickered in his lips. He wanted to go on thinking such thoughts but the eerie screech of some night bird startled him out of his reverie. It was getting late and he hadn't caught any fish yet. Hurriedly, lowering his old worn-out net from his shoulders and neatly folding it and making two handfuls of it, Haren advanced to unfurl the net only to stop short in his tracks. Down the ribbony village alley, which seemed now to be floating in a mass of fog, Goroi was coming that way. On seeing him come much earlier than his usual time, an irritated Haren started folding up his net. Gathering his bamboo scoop, creel and small bamboo basket and tying them to his waist, he was starting down the shortcut when he noticed that today Goroi seemed to be walking almost at a snail's pace, very slow but steady. It took him a long time to reach the Ow tree. What's wrong with the boy? Curious, Haren tip-toed carefully over the dew-wet fallen leaves and advanced toward Goroi. To his utter amazement, he saw that even in this freezing cold Goroi was naked, completely naked!

That afternoon, Goroi had been sitting gloomily under a mango tree, thinking of his mother. Suddenly, the village head's milky-white cow, which he had helped to tend along with Dhaniram, came that way. Stopping near him, she started to lick him. Having left the village head's service now, he was always saddened to see these cows. Unmindfully, he began to stroke the white cow. Dhaniram and a few other cowherds were watching from a distance. All of a sudden, as the mischievous thought struck him, he blurted out in his high-pitched voice, 'You see, that is how the water spirit must have fondled your mother.'

Each word uttered by Dhaniram pierced the depths of Goroi's soul like the pricks of a thorny fish and made him feel like a magur fish cut and salted alive. Yet he sat unheeding, still stroking the white cow. But further inciting comments ignited his normally subdued but hot temper. Suddenly, running at great speed towards Dhaniram, he dealt him a blow on the right arm with the stick he held in his hand, then another and another till he had hit Dhaniram good and proper. Seeing him attack Dhaniram, the rest of the cowherds surrounded him. On hearing the commotion, the village head's farm labourers also ran that way. Without stopping to listen to Goroi, they all started raining blows on him. Unable to ward off their blows, he fell to the ground almost unconscious and began drooling at the mouth. Someone even pulled off the loincloth he wore tied around his waist. As he lay in their midst in his rough, ugly nakedness, they formed a circle around him, all laughing with a sort of unholy glee.

As he lay unable to move, Dhaniram came to check if there was life yet in the bloody and battered body. As he moved closer, Dhaniram seemed to get the smell of raw fish. One by one, after Dhaniram, the rest of the cowherds too moved close and all of them found him smelling of raw fish. Now there remained no doubt in their minds that he was the son of the 'Bak', the water spirit. After a while, on seeing him move, the lads ran homewards all chiming in tune, 'Goroi the spirit's son, Goroi the spirit's son'. Before running off, Dhaniram flung Goroi's loincloth out of reach, into the high branch of a mango tree.

On moonlit nights, Haren was accustomed to seeing Goroi wandering about the lakeside near the Ow tree. That was nothing new for him. But the sight of Goroi, naked and injured, with deep welts running down his back, was an unnerving sight for him. It looked as if someone had cut welts on a live fish before frying it. A shiver shook Haren's whole frame as he caught sight of Goroi's wounds. His face was badly swollen and the blood had dried in streaks under his nose. He seemed to look even uglier today. Who would say that it was in beautiful Padumi's womb that this ugly child had taken form, grown hands, grown feet.

'Pitai!'

Suddenly, breaking the silence of the night, the piteous cry rang out. For an instant, it seemed as if the soft waves of the lake, the wind blowing over that lake and the light bamboo leaves fluttering in that wind had all been stilled by that cry. Looking down into the depths of the water was Goroi, calling out,

'Pitai . . .!'

At once, realising the reason behind Goroi's strange wanderings, Haren felt apprehensive. Father! Who was his father? People say he is the spirit's son. When they say so in front of him, he feels a strange mirth. On the other hand, old Pabhoi claimed that Goroi is her Tikheroo's son. But how could Goroi be the son of Tikheroo? A few days after Goroi's birth, the doctor from the nearby garden had secretly told him of Tikheroo's problem. After trying many a remedy, Tikheroo had come to the doctor too for a cure but the doctor had not been able to help him. The doctor stated that Tikheroo was incapable of becoming a father.

With much hope in his heart, Haren had rowed the boat to the lonely stretch of the lake. He had then hit Tikheroo behind the head with the oar. After writhing in agony for a while, Tikheroo's lifeless body had become still at the bottom of the boat. Binding the body with an old net, Haren had buried it in the marshes near the cremation ground. But, after killing Tikheroo, Haren could never approach Padumi again. Her husband's death not only took a toll on her beauty, but also stole away sleep from her eyes for ever. On hearing of Tikheroo's death from Haren, Padumi had not believed it at first. But when, braving the storm, she ran to the lakeside only to see thousands of fish floating on the lake surface, she stood still, shocked. She could never again shut those eyes that she had then opened wide in terror and agony.

Though he failed to make her his own, the sight of her swelling belly nevertheless filled him with a kind of joy. Maybe not in his wedded wife, but still his child was taking form inside Padumi.

'Pitai!'

Advancing a few steps from under the tree to the lakeside, Goroi once again cried out. Like the moaning notes of a flute, his heartrending cry gave a twist to Haren's heart. The fount of love so long lying dried up in Haren seemed suddenly to well up with Goroi's soulful cry. About to call out, Haren stopped. Instead of his voice, a deep sigh escaped him.

Standing dangerously close to the steep bank of the lake, Goroi repeated his cry in a barely audible voice. Each moment seemed to pass slowly, as if unsure of itself. Suddenly, with one last shuddering call, which seemed to rend both the air and the water, Goroi jumped into the lake. On seeing Goroi jump in, Haren too ran that way. Looking down, he saw a well of darkness in the moonlit water. A great many waves were circling that bit of darkness. Haren was aware that this part of the lake was deep. It was a part washed by strong waves such that a full-grown elephant with its rider would not get a footing. It was here that the boy had jumped in.

Throwing down his net, Haren too jumped into the dark

depths of the lake. The surface water of the lake was washed with faint moonlight but the depths were dark, and getting darker. In those dark depths mauled by the waves, Haren desperately searched for the boy, groping here and there. But there was no trace of Goroi. Still, as long as he was able to hold his breath, he searched for his son in that village of sleeping fish, crushing under his weight their numerous homes with their surrounding greenery of underwater plants. He even lay quietly on the bed of the lake, trying to catch the sound of the thrashing of an arm or leg of his son. But no, nothing, no sound came to his ears. All he seemed to hear in the water were the deep sighs of the orphaned fish.

Disappointed, Haren ascended to the surface for a breath of air. Even before he could reach the surface, a pair of hands grabbed his legs. Haren found himself unable to escape that strong mysterious grasp. The more he tried, the more strongly those hands held him. In desperation and fear, he shouted out. His breathless, agonised scream only raised a few bubbles in the water.

Feeling that his long wait for his father had ended at last, in the dark depths of the water, Goroi held him to his breast in such a strong embrace that Haren was stilled.

And then the mirthful fish swam around the embracing figures of father and son as, naked and stiff, they whirled round and round, descending further into the depths of the lake.

* * *

Translated from the original Assamese by Mitali Goswami and published in The Water Spirit and Other Stories, *Harper Perennial, an imprint of Harper Collins Publishers, India, 2015*

BOOTS

Nilutpal Baruah
Translated by Rashmi Baruah

Bedo Bora bought a pair of boots.

He got them at the most expensive showroom in the shopping mall. And went home with the triumphant expression of a Samurai warrior back from an intense war at the frontier.

They were expensive.

Shiny black leather boots with several steel studs on them.

They had an aura about them.

And all at once, Bedo Bora was not Bedo Bora any more. He transformed instantly into a Magadhi prostitute. Skilled. As sharp as an arrow. A long nail on her little finger scratched the royal prince, hitherto untouched by the sun, on his way back from the gurukul after completing his education. Forearm, chest, stomach, thigh . . .! The boots transformed Bedo Bora, broke him, built him, melted him, dried him out . . .

It was not as if he did not own any shoes. He did. He did

own a pair. It was not even as though the boots were going to suit him. They would not. This, he was sure of.

Bedo Bora was a gaunt man. At first glance he seemed to have no personality at all. Someone who would easily get lost in a crowd. Swarthy. Dim eyes. Feeble voice. Going by the average size in the Indian subcontinent, his organ could just about be called a penis.

People said Bedo Bora was a foot fetishist. He was fascinated by women's feet. He would keep staring at everyone's feet, male or female. Most people would be disconcerted at the sight of him staring at their feet when he met them for the first time.

Bedo Bora was not a foot fetishist.

Bedo Bora was not a foot fetishist. He did not have a sexual fascination with feet.

Even when they had been sexually active, he had never licked or sucked or kissed his wife Nidhima Kashyap's feet. For that would have been a vile outcome of causality. If he had, that might have been just a reflex action.

(There was no way he could be submissive.)

Bedo Bora had never given her feet a place in their foreplay either.

Nidhima Kashyap Bora had beautiful feet. Beautiful enough to inspire jealousy. She took good care of them too. (However, Nidhi Kashyap gave more importance to her womb than to her feet.)

Rumour was that Bedo Bora noticed people's feet first.

The whole thing was quite unpalatable.

But as his actions were not sexual or criminal in nature, no one had lodged a complaint against him.

The issue just dissipated into the universe like a simple, innocent, childlike and baseless inquisitiveness.

Bedo Bora's pet subject was actually people's shoes.

Hidden deep within his heart was a shoe infatuation. It ran through his blood, through his veins.

Everyone thought he had a foot fetish.

(Their neighbour Ragini Saikia respected this habit of his, irrespective of whether it was good or bad.

Ragini Saikia spent a large part of her college-teacher husband's salary on her feet.

Regular pedicures, waxing, massage, expensive nail paints . . .

And, after that, she would put on a figure-hugging black skirt.

A pair of red shoes.

And then she would go out, exhibiting her feet like a stock of tempting eggplants being taken to the market.

As though they were not feet, but a sharp Katana sword.

White like the inside of a bottle gourd, her feet were her trump card.

Her feet had wounded many a king and a prince.

Others bowed before her feet like slaves when given a firm command.

It gave Ragini Saikia inexplicable joy when Bedo Bora stared at her feet.)

It had not been long since Bedo Bora had learnt to love himself. His parents had named him Bedai. The villagers too used to call him Bedai. He felt an extreme distaste towards the name. And an equal feeling of inferiority.

When he took admission in the school that was run from the local church, his name was stated to be Bedai Bora. God knows what the nun from Kerala heard or understood, but she wrote his name with the English letter corresponding to the 'Bh' sound. He had to spend his days in high school as Bhedo Bora.

His self-esteem turned into a larva that coiled itself up deep within its cocoon.

He received a scholarship from the Sonai Kalita Trust to study in a far-off town. When Akangsha Sonowal, an English-medium school product, called out to him there, 'Hey Vedaa . . . listen!', it was as though his self-esteem became a lemon sapling that sprouted deep inside him and started spreading its branches.

Akangsha's spartan-warrior-like sandals with their leather straps wrapped around her calves made him give her everything uncomplainingly. His lab records, notes . . .

But he dared not offer her his heart, nor did she ask him to.

Bedo Bora lived a modest life.

Extremely modest . . .

He had an uneventful childhood.

His parents' daily, noisy coupling to fulfil his father's hope of another child! The tussle every night between his reluctant mother and blunt, enthusiastic father. The creaking of the old bed his mother had brought with her trousseau.

Sweat-coated objections permeated the two-roomed small log house.

In this dimly lit house, Bedo Bora's shoe-hedonism gradually intensified.

To play the role of a messenger, his father had hired a pair of ornamental sandals from the costume store . . . that was his first encounter with an image of a shoe. Bedo Bora hid the shoes, which were decorated with small stones and a golden lace.

For a very long time, he even slept with them in his bed.

There was a celebration the day Bedo Bora received his first pair of shoes. His father took him early in the morning to a market far away. Usually, they just took the vegetables to sell in the weekly market. But that day there were two sacks of a rare variety of rice too.

The squealing of piglets being sold, the non-stop advertisements of the local medicine seller . . .

Luridly coloured sweetmeats being fried as the bubbling oil sizzled . . .

The fragrance of jasmine wafting from the bearded perfume seller . . .

The smell of raw bananas filled his senses as Bedo Bora sat waiting for all the rice to be sold.

Munching on the biscuit his father managed to hand him at one point, he looked beseechingly at each of the traders.

Every look was a plea.

A prayer thick with fervour.

The entreaty of a slave willing to be sold.

It took a lot of pleading and bargaining before the Muslim trader sold them a pair of canvas shoes, that too at the price of two bags of rice. And, besides, he also took their unsold ridge gourd and sponge gourd.

A father swollen with pride at having bought his only son a pair of shoes, and the elated son transformed into a victorious Cossack . . .! They were homeward bound on a creaking cycle, down the narrow, winding cow-trail.

His father could not wear shoes. His feet were deformed. The big toes stuck out, which wore out his rubber slippers quickly on this terrain. It was only when he went somewhere that he wore them.

(A pair of sandals from the Bronze Age was discovered during archaeological excavations in Greece. It might have dated back to nearly 5,000 years BCE. Apparently, the formation of people's feet began to change when the idea of shoes materialised. The shape and size of the feet of human fossils pointed to the status of the person. Slaves and peasants had broad feet with crooked toes. On the other hand, the feet of the aristocracy were unblemished.

Bedo Bora's father's feet were undoubtedly those of a slave.)

By the time Bedo Bora realised that people ate three meals a day and that each meal had its own distinctive name, his feet had outgrown the black canvas shoes. His big toes had poked holes in them. Bedo Bora applied some tar on that area and prayed earnestly—this time, for his feet to become small.

(As small as was necessary for Chinese women to be considered beautiful. Aristocratic ladies of China used to wear wooden shoes during the period of the Five Dynasties and Seven Kingdoms of the Song Dynasty to keep their feet small. And their feet did become tiny. But it made the women sick. It made them lose their balance. Groaning with unbearable pain, the small-footed women later suffered from psychological disorders.)

Eating nothing but pumpkin tendrils, jackfruit seeds when they were in season, or raw plantains when they grew, the growing boy Bedo Bora finally saw an expensive pair of shoes for the first time . . .

. . . It was during this time that Babul had dropped out from class eight and joined the militant outfit ULFA. The thick-set Babul's body changed suddenly.

Whiling away his time at the crossroads, Babul, by now a regular card-player, bought a RX100 motorcycle. Bedo Bora's eyes nearly popped out at seeing the denim-clad Babul wearing a pair of Woodland shoes. He even allowed Bedo Bora to touch them.

Bedo Bora inhaled the crisp smell of new leather to his heart's content!

Later, he saw his college classmate, Utpal, wearing a similar pair.

Utpal, who had once proposed to Nidhi Kashyap.

Nidhi had not responded.

On the contrary, one afternoon, at the head of a deserted corridor, it was Nidhi who had proposed to Bedo Bora.

(It was actually an invitation to her womb.) Gazing with rapt attention at her shiny black pump shoes, Bedo Bora fortified himself after the shock.

He understood instantly—this love was not an impetuous one. It was calculated. An easy way to arrive at the perfect equation. The brilliant Bedo Bora's outstanding marks were all it required for this love to materialise.

It astonished everyone that the beautiful daughter of a blue-blooded administrative officer was the lover of the unattractive, inaudible Bedo Bora.

Nidhi Kashyap was neither too sharp nor dull.

If someone were to ask her at an intimate moment, 'Nidhi, what is your aim in life?', she would reply in the blink of an eye, 'To become a mother!' To bear a child in her womb.

That was all.

The sinuous Nidhi Kashyap of the hour-glass figure wanted only to be a mother.

That is why she had selected Bedo Bora, for his superior sperm.

(That was how it happened . . . Nidhi Kashyap readied her fallopian tubes on their wedding night.)

And that was what Bedo Bora's and Nidhi Kashyap's love-talk was about . . . Nidhi Kashyap would steer the conversation towards pregnancy every time.

'Normal delivery would be best. A caesarean can create complications later.'

'If only we had one of those foot-operated wooden pestles . . . That's how you set the baby perfectly in the womb. No problems during the delivery.'

'If the mother eats half a dry gooseberry and uses the other half to shape the baby's eyebrows, the baby will grow up to have perfect arched brows.'

'You know Bedo . . . my first child will be a girl! Sharma uncle checked my horoscope today.'

'The baby's nails will fall off on their own if I blow on them first thing in the morning, before I even brush my teeth. I am so scared of nail cutters.'

Bedo Bora was very sure—if someone were to write

about their love story, they would definitely title it 'Bedo and Nidhi's Journey to the Womb'.

Once, he had mentioned that they would go to Armenia for their honeymoon. (The world's oldest footwear had been excavated in Armenia. A ceramic bowl, the horns of a goat and a pair of shoe-shaped leather objects.) But it did not materialise.

One night, Bedo Bora saw the boots of the State for the first time.

Gleaming black ones.

Heavy, blunt boots.

Stub-toed.

Babul of ULFA was beating up small traders with a thick bamboo stick in the market, for they were not coughing up money for the organisation. From the vegetable seller to the one selling cattle, no one escaped his wrath.

One night, a panting Babul dashed into his house. The military had surrounded the entire village.

A sturdy soldier stood with his boot on Babul's battered head as he lay on the floor.

A thin stream of blood trickled down his nose. A single movement, and several other pairs of boots stomped on Babul.

Shivering under the bed, Bedo Bora saw these boots of the State from a very close distance. They were dark in colour, heavy, with metal rims.

Ruthless.

Cold.

(Later, Babul became an informer for the army. With a dark cloth tied around his face, it was he who pointed out

Charu and his gang when they were hiding near one of the islands that appeared seasonally on the river. At the end of a night-long gun fight, the police wrapped the dead bodies of Charu and his mates in bamboo mats and threw them on the school grounds at the edge of the village.)

Gradually, Bedo Bora was drawn deeper into the world of shoes.

An infinite cosmos, a shoe universe filled with the endless illusion of reality.

A young Latin American woman, sitting on one end of a stone bench in Lodhi Garden, talking animatedly on the phone . . . She was telling her sister about their father's new girlfriend . . . The smell of goat cheese wafted strongly from her body. She was wearing a pair of bison-hide red moccasins. . .

The young Kumaoni woman who entered the Mango showroom in South Extension . . . She drew her feet in as though to hide her battered rexine sandals on the sparkling marble floor. . .

The young man from Ghana, wearing Veldskoen shoes . . . He used to sell drugs in the area near Satya Niketan . . . The police had taken him to the station, making him sit in between them on their motorbike . . . He was probably not out of jail as yet.

The Gujjar daughter-in-law on Tilak Puri Road . . . Her husband had pushed her off their balcony . . . A pair of pump shoes with buckles lay by the body that had burst open . . . She had been about to leave for her mother's house after a fight with her husband. . .

Guniya . . . Guniya . . . The young deaf and mute woman

from the slums in the jungles of Mehrauli . . . Someone had thrown her body under a margosa tree after raping her! Her lower body was uncovered . . . Dotted with clotted blood.

Nearby lay her sandals cut out from a tyre . . .

Over the last couple of days, a young man had been bothering Bedo Bora's daughter.

Whistling, lewd gestures . . .

He used to shout out obscenities as he sped past on his motorbike.

He paid no heed even if Bedo Bora was sitting in the verandah. There was nothing menacing about Bedo Bora in any case.

Bedo Bora put on his boots.

And became the State.

He stepped out.

PUHOR

Ashamoni Neog
Translated by Rashmi Baruah

'Best wishes on your special day' ... 'Many, many happy returns of the day, Puhor' ... Warm, flowery birthday greetings had been pouring into her inbox since morning. Cakes and various gifts arrived, ordered online by her friends. Emotionless. Impersonal wishes. Copy-pasted from somewhere, and forwarded to her.

Nikhil, her fiancé, had come by with a red velvet cake. But god knows she felt no joy. She should have been happy in the company of such a caring, attentive man. She should have been. But she couldn't make herself feel that way. On his way out, Nikhil gazed deeply into her eyes and carefully pressed a gaily wrapped package into her hands. She opened it passively. Meticulously woven in wool, in her favourite colour, was a dream-catcher!

Dream! Dreamer!

Aah ... like Lennon, the dreamer, Ashwash too used to wear glasses. Eternally running hand in hand with his dreams, Ashwash looked like a philosopher in those glasses. In the guise of seriousness, though, he was in reality nothing but a naughty mouse. Curious! Frisky! No, no . . . what was she thinking of? Nikhil had driven all the way from Jalukbari, through the massive traffic jam at Maligaon, to Uzanbazar, just to spend some time with her. But here she was, hovering on the edge of Rumi's field, beyond all ideas of wrongdoing and right-doing.

'Puhor, are you OK? Are you feeling unwell?' Nikhil asked, sounding concerned.

Startled, Puhor dragged herself out of her reverie and, trying to paste a smile on her face, said, 'I'm fine. Just a little headache . . .'

'You're under too much pressure at work. Why do you need to work on your birthday?'

'Can't be helped . . . March is the end of the financial year, you know how it is,' Puhor lied blandly.

How could she give Nikhil an inkling of the tempest raging inside her? Could she tell him of her yearning for Ashwash, or that she had decided to go and look for him? More than her, it was actually Nikhil who had left no stone unturned to search for Ashwash, in the belief that it would make her happy. He accompanied her everywhere she wished to go in her quest to find Ashwash. But there had to be a limit to his patience too. How could she keep dragging everyone into this? She was going to search for Ashwash on her own after work today.

'Should I drop you at your office?' Nikhil asked again, worriedly.

'No, it's OK. I can manage. You go.' Puhor smiled thinly.

* * *

It was her ego that had made her block Ashwash's number a few months ago. But later, climbing over that nearly insurmountable mountain, when she had tentatively tried to call him one day, a mechanical voice had answered, 'The number you are calling is currently not reachable. Please try again later.'

Puhor had tried. Finding Ashwash's phone switched off for the third day in a row, she had turned up at his flat. The leather sofa was missing. The sofa where they used to fall asleep after working late into the night. The swing-chair and bean bag on the balcony, where they used to sit with beer bottles, cursing everyone under the sun, were gone too.

There was nothing left behind. The empty floor and the bare walls waited mutely to be soothed by a ray of light. Like the empty flat, her insides too became a void.

A strangeness took over after Ashwash had left.

It was on one of those turbulent days that she had agreed to marry Nikhil. She gave him her word. Impetuously but ardently.

She needed Nikhil to fill her emptiness, the void inside. The same way she had found a support in Ashwash years after Reni's disappearance.

Reni. Her friend from their university days.

Reni. Her first love.

* * *

That was an old story . . . it must have been around eight years ago.

Gazing affectionately into her swollen, red eyes, Reni had patted her on the head and said, 'Idiot! You have been crying all night about such a silly thing? I will take care of your admission fees. Tell your mother not to worry about these things as long as I am around. Let me see if I can also manage to organise some money for your brother's studies.'

Reni gave the money for Puhor's admission, the money that she had been saving to apply to a foreign institution.

Though a student of psychology herself, Reni used to sleepily write out social science notes for Puhor late into the night. Puhor sometimes hid a grin on seeing her crooked handwriting. Now, looking back, she felt that it was eerily similar to someone else's handwriting. Who knew where Reni had managed to track down the books Puhor needed! What a pure current of love and warmth they used to swim in!

Reni would find mention even in the limited time that Puhor managed to speak to her mother over the hostel phone. Her mother used to say, 'Reni is so caring. I would have got you married to her if she had been a boy.'

When Puhor told Reni about this later, she jokingly said, 'Oh, that means I shall have to change my sex.' And they both laughed, louder perhaps than required. It was in hindsight that Puhor now understood that the laughter was an attempt to hide her true feelings.

Countless boys at the university had sent love notes and bouquets of roses to Puhor. Those gifts triggered much envy among the other girls from their hostel. But Reni and she would read the letters doubled over with laughter.

'We don't like your tendencies.' Noticing their growing closeness, a few seniors from their hostel had given them a warning.

Things became complicated, however, the day Arup from the second year pulled her into a corner of the classroom and told her, 'You are a girl. Try to behave like one. Behave as a girl normally would. You must have already heard about Gautam and Prakash . . . and still you continue with this nonsense? Weren't you Pronoy's girlfriend? So how did Reni drop into the equation? Are you bi, you bitch? Or has Reni entrapped you? It's better for you to stay away from her. Else you too will be expelled in no time. Remember, you have been warned. I am still fond of you, so I am telling you this as a well-wisher. Beware!'

As he walked away after warning her, she wanted to whisper to his retreating back, 'Reni is just my best friend.' But she paused.

Was she really her best friend?

What lay beyond being one's best friend?

A soulmate?

And beyond that. . .?

The moment she started thinking about it, a mild tingle ran down Puhor's spine.

The tingles were apprehensions of unintentional love. Days passed. The tingles grew severe. Society, friends, her mother, Reni—whom to cast aside and whom to hold on to? She was caught in an unrelenting game of tug of war within herself. Society won. Hesitation triumphed. Love lost. Like it always does. Reni was brave, but not Puhor. She began to avoid Reni. Was she avoiding Reni, or, in reality, running away from her own self? Her own unarticulated feelings had given birth to a volcano within.

She discovered herself in the debris left behind by the hot, destructive, molten lava the day Reni suddenly approached her from the back in the university canteen and planted a kiss on her cheek. The hundreds of sharp looks directed at them shook Puhor's heart. 'Stay away from me,' she screamed, in a voice that trembled. Reni reached out, as though to ask her what had happened so suddenly. But, without hesitation, she screamed again, 'Fuck off, you fucking lesbian! Don't touch me!'

Everyone had been waiting for just this truth to unfold.

Like the rush for freshly slaughtered meat at the butcher's on Sundays, a section of people surged towards Reni.

Others stared at her as if at a strange creature no one had ever seen before. Some abused her with vile words, some even spat on her. The university suddenly became a jungle.

Puhor fainted. When she regained consciousness, she found herself lying on the bed in her hostel room, with a few senior students on guard around her. 'She was half-mad in any case. Talking of queer people all the time. She should have been sent away from the university long ago.' 'She touched you in places where she was not supposed to, didn't she? The bloody wildcat should have her rough edges pounded smooth in a mortar and pestle. Why didn't you stay away from her when you were warned?' Hour after hour they came to sit with her. One by one, to commiserate, to express sorrow, to find enjoyment in talking of taboos.

It was as though a spear had pierced her heart, and scraped her insides. She felt trapped in a maze of her own creation. The more she learnt of the atrocities on Reni, the deeper her anguish became. She froze. Towards nightfall, when it was time for Reni to leave the hostel, and she saw her red-rimmed eyes, suicidal thoughts crossed Puhor's mind for the very first time. That was the last time Puhor saw Reni. She simply disappeared.

She never got to know where Reni's parents had taken her.

Puhor was in the grip of a very high fever by late evening. When she became delirious, they took her to the hospital, and then, after a few days, she had to be taken home.

She would wake up every night, sweating and restless, from the same nightmare.

The university canteen. A dim light flickering in its centre. Surrounded by a dense, dark jungle. A deep post-midnight darkness. The howls of jackals sporadically rending the sky. Suddenly, countless students, leaping like frenzied beasts, rush from the middle of the jungle and crowd around the canteen. As though they are waiting eagerly for something. Gradually, their murmurs grow louder. She too moves forward to see what is happening. Abruptly, a pair of bearded demonic dark shadowy figures with red eyes overtake her. Her body is wracked by tremors at the sight. Triumphantly, they drag a wounded figure to the centre of the canteen. The other students rush forward to look at the day's fresh catch. Their shrill shouts make the environment even ghostlier. The sight of the scratched, lacerated, bleeding flesh hanging in shreds from the bones of the mangled figure makes Puhor's guts curl up and pushes her to the point of throwing up. The figure's sad cry for help pierces Puhor's soul and drains her. Suddenly, the figure lifts its head and stares miserably at Puhor with tear-filled eyes. She is shocked—even the pain and the indistinct light cannot conceal their identity. Reni's eyes. Puhor's Reni.

Each time, she woke up with a start at this point, trembling uncontrollably, and then let out a piercing scream and vomited violently. Eager to wipe out the memories of her guilt, she would scribble furiously on a piece of paper and then tear it up into countless tiny pieces in a frenzy, choking all the while. She wanted to tell her mother, or a relative ... someone ... anyone, the truth about her relationship with Reni. But she could not bring Reni's name to her lips. Sometimes she would sit silently in a corner of the house, contemplating what could have been—what if the story could have had a different ending, one that might have left her with a better feeling. When she thought about those happier times, she would burst out laughing. Or break into tears without any obvious reason. The wall of patience and steadfastness that her mother and brother were barely managing to hold up had collapsed. Teary-eyed, they would pick up after her—things that she had left strewn everywhere—and even clean the floor that she would keep soiling. She had virtually no memory of the year that passed. The following year, she recalled her brother taking her to the psychiatrist Anindita Gogoi. She was asked to maintain a diary and record the minutest of details of her day—what time she woke up, what she had eaten for breakfast, whether she exercised, whether she had watered the plants, what she spoke about with people, etc. In the first month, the pages remained blank. Gradually, she started to write a few things at her mother's and brother's insistence, and on the psychiatrist's orders. She found these very tedious. Initially, she hated the psychiatrist for forcing her to write, but now she had come to accept the renowned Anindita Gogoi as her mentor. On Gogoi's encouragement, she joined Shuwash, an NGO, where she herself was the chief advisor.

The chaos inside her head began to subside, though the past did make its presence felt at times. That was when Ashwash had come into her life, to rescue her from her disquietude, as it were. He taught her self-acceptance. She never had to explain anything to him, it was as though he understood her soul. Working with Ashwash for the queer community, she found that the heavy stone weighing down her heart had become lighter.

Only once . . . if she could meet Reni just once, to seek her forgiveness . . . Puhor mused while driving to work, as she did even today. First Reni, now Ashwash. . .whom should she go looking for? And where? 'Ahh. . . where are you hiding, Ashwash? Why?' Puhor shouted, masking her voice with a blast from the car horn. As soon as she entered her cabin, she threw her bag on the table and sat with her head in her hands.

It was exactly two years to the date, on her birthday, that Anindita Baidew had brought a young man to her office. By then, five years had passed since the incident with Reni. But thoughts of the events still kept bothering her. Sometimes grief would choke her throat and hold her heart in a vice-like grip, turning her eyes red. And, instantly, she would become mute, just gazing unwaveringly into the distance. Sometimes, she would be startled on hearing a word that Reni had often used, or on spotting a subtle gesture Reni used to make. She would jump to her feet—maybe Reni was nearby? That day, the sight of the young man with Anindita Baidew made her feel as though a thousand yellow flowers had suddenly bloomed all at once inside her body. Short hair and beard, trimmed smartly. A well-built body. The man stood in front of her, wearing a light-pink collarless shirt and a pair of dark-blue trousers. Sloping eyebrows, deep eyes that could absorb a thousand sorrows, the cute yet naughty lopsided grin—it was like she could see Reni a thousand times in front of her eyes at once. While she was fruitlessly trying to bring this sudden awakening of her sense organs under control, Baidew said, 'Puhor, this is Ashwash Barua. He too works for an NGO like ours . . . Asha. Ashwash handles all the awareness programmes and trains others too. You will be able to learn a lot from him. You keep saying that you need more work, if you stick to Ashwash you will never run out of things to do. And Ashwash, this is Puhor, a very bright and promising member of our organisation.'

That was how they had first met. Puhor couldn't have imagined at that moment that the name 'Ashwash' would take such deep root in her heart. She had left no stone unturned to search for Ashwash over the past month, yet she could not even find an organisation named Asha. She was surprised. She asked Anindita Baidew about his whereabouts countless times, made innumerable calls, but could not find him.

Ashwash had never taken her to his office even when she had insisted. Asha's office was chaotic in comparison to Shuwash, there was some renovation happening, the time was not right—he always came up with excuses. When the time came, the man himself disappeared.

She was jolted out of her thoughts—her colleagues had got a cake and were singing 'Happy birthday Puhor' loudly. She managed to push thoughts of Ashwash away and joined in the celebrations.

The sun began to set. But she did not receive even a wish from Ashwash. Once, she had asked Ashwash as they were working at Shuwash, 'How come you never tell me anything about your family? Tell me, please. I want to go to your house one day.'

In reply, he had just sung the immortal song 'moi eti jajabor . . . I am a wanderer' and burst out laughing. Now how was Puhor to find this wanderer?

Packing up for the day, she decided to drive by the Brahmaputra. Sometimes, a fear would pop up in her head: 'I hope nothing untoward has happened to Ashwash.' But she would calm herself the very next moment, 'No, that's impossible.'

She parked her car near the river, in their special spot, where they used to sit and talk for hours on end. Ashwash would bring her here quite frequently. They used to sing too, at the top of their voices, along with the college kids who would jam there with their guitars, rattles and cajons.

With the realisation of her love and respect for him growing, Puhor was waiting for Ashwash at their favourite restaurant Hakuna Matata one evening. That day, unexpectedly, he had brought a special person along and introduced her—'Puhor, this is my very old friend Upoma.' So much meaning could be hidden in a single sentence.

Thoughts, words, actions. The blush that spread across his ears and cheeks, his lowered eyes, the sudden urge to scratch the tip of his nose—all of these spoke loudly to her what he was trying to convey.

Rattled by the unspoken emotions, she hurriedly exited from the half-eaten dinner. Going down in the lift, she cried, whereupon a man offered her a white handkerchief. It was Nikhil.

Today, she could see a couple of youngsters practising their music on the river-bank.

They were beginning to sing Bhupen Hazarika's 'Tumi notun purush. . . tumi notun nari. . . onagoto dinor jagroto prohori. . . you are a new man. . .you are a new woman. . . you will be an alert sentinel in the coming days. . .'

Once, when they were sitting idly, Puhor had asked him in fun, 'If you were to choose between the two words—Asha and Shuwash—which one would you choose?'

He thought for a while and said, 'I will not choose Asha or hope, nor spread Shuwash . . . fragrance. I will spread Puhor . . . light.' This was accompanied by an inscrutable smile.

Pointing at the top of a hill in the distance, on the other side of the river, he said, 'Can you see that peak there, where it looks as though the sun is almost setting? I wish to spread puhor there, so that dawn breaks early.'

Something stirred in her memory when she recalled these words. She sat up straight and started driving quickly in the direction of the setting sun.

She crossed a big bridge and traversed a couple of unpaved roads until a winding road finally led her to the top of the hill. And there she saw a massive five-storied building, with a huge neon signboard saying: The Puhor Foundation.

An unknown sensation shook her to the core. She could not ascertain whether she was feeling hot or cold. As she opened her car door, the doorman came forward quickly. Not just him, it was as though everyone in the organisation had been simply waiting for her to turn up.

A faintly familiar young woman came forward to offer her a glass of water. When she came close, Puhor realised it was Upoma, but she was wearing a badge stating she was Panchoi 10. She hurriedly took a few sips of water and was about to ask Upoma aka Panchoi a question, when a tall young man appeared and led her to a cabin at the front of the long building. About to ask him a question too, she glanced at his name on the badge and was astonished. It said Ashwash 12.

She was mystified. Where was the Ashwash she knew?

She lost count of the number of Panchois and Ashwashs she passed on the way to the cabin. She saw people sitting in the rows of chairs lined up in the long building. Some were reading newspapers, while others were watching documentaries on animals on the TV. The place had the appearance of a hospital.

Her eyes were suddenly drawn to a photo on the wall, of Anindita Baidew and Ashwash. Below it was written, 'Treatment at atomic level, without sharing our identity'.

Her curiosity increased. What treatment was the picture referring to?

Why hadn't Ashwash told her about this foundation? Why had he named it Puhor? Was it named for her?

Where was she to find the answers to these questions?

She felt like calling Nikhil immediately to tell him about her strange and weird discovery, and that perhaps she was on the verge of finding Ashwash finally. The moment she met him, she would give him two tight slaps. And only after that would she enquire about him. She might not be his lover, but she was definitely his friend. She had the right to hit him.

By then they had reached the door of a cabin. The nameplate on the door said Director. Ashwash 12 held the door open for her. She entered to find the room empty. Puzzled, she looked around, and noticed an envelope on the desk. Curiously enough, it said, 'To Dear Puhor'.

The handwriting was familiar. It was Ashwash's.

She tore it open at once and began reading the letter inside.

'Puhor, I know you will come here one day in search of me. The time has finally come, Puhor. This was my organisation, Asha. And now it is Puhor. I hand over this Puhor to you today. Please accept this as a small gift.

'Please forgive me. When Anindita Baidew approached me to treat you, I fell in love with you once again. But how could I disrupt the dignity of the organisation that I had created myself. Protocol demands that a doctor cannot ever fall in love with a patient. Nor can a doctor disclose their full identity to their patient. But I do not exist without loving you! I cannot put up an act in your presence. I used Upoma just as a pawn to distance you from my life.

'I am leaving the country. We shall meet again someday. Hopefully, in a parallel universe.

'In no man's land . . .

Ashwash I, alias Reni'

THE COURTYARD

Debasish Buragohain

Translated by Rashmi Baruah and
Syeda Shaheen Jeenat Suhailey

There were no clouds in the sky then, nor are there any now. The towering areca nut trees filled up the courtyard, letting just a fistful of moonlight through. The giant areca nut grove has now disappeared without a trace. Fifty trees had once been felled to pitch a tent for Roop's grandfather's funeral. It was only after the stumps were uprooted and thrown away that adequate space was found to accommodate all the villagers. But just as the moonlight brightened gradually over the courtyard, so did the heat of the sun! Like the courtyard, the house too lost its overhead canopy.

The areca nut grove grew sparse. But the under-storey layer remained as neat as ever, with the extra growth trimmed. Needless to say, the sinuous betel creepers wound themselves up around the areca nut trees. Roop's father had inherited his own father's green thumb. Whatever he planted, no matter where, the plants flourished. People said,

'Like father, like son', but Roop's father's stature surpassed his grandfather's. If his grandfather was akin to a huge mango tree, his father was a lofty banyan. But a sudden stroke forced even a personage like him to depart from this mortal plane in an instant. For the next two days, newspaper journalists and Assam's most eminent personalities, among others, kept pouring into their house. Roop's dishevelled mother fell wailing to the ground in the middle of the courtyard. That was when the courtyard was cleared for the first time. To make space for the public funeral for Roop's father, the entire areca nut grove was uprooted and discarded. Obviously, the betel climbers ceased to exist as well.

What was Roop's mother but a creeper herself? She had been a parasitic plant once, dependent on her husband. By that calculation, she too should have wilted away. Roop and his mother's future should have been like a blank page, across which a pen had been drawn repeatedly till it lay tattered.

But that was not the case.

People are not trees. Even when the devastating hammer of time throws people into the darkness of a bottomless pit, their strong desire to survive remains. Responsibility gives unbelievable strength to people. They fight, and win, with the combined strength of every cell of the body.

Roop's mother didn't lose. The woman who had entered her marriage like untouched, freshly fallen night-flowering jasmines now grew as strong as devil's grass. The remaining mulch of the betel creepers turned into fertiliser for the devil's grass that now covered every nook and corner of the courtyard. The courtyard found relief from the sun's scorching heat and the sticky mud that the rain carried in its bosom.

Roop was seven at the time.

'Why are you cleaning the yard, Roop?' Roop's mother found him trying to clear a patch of grass from the courtyard, with a hoe that he could barely hold as it was taller than him.

'I'm building a cricket pitch, Ma. I will play cricket with Konmoina, Munu and the others. You can watch from the veranda.'

'No, no . . . you don't need to play cricket! What if the ball comes flying and hits you in the face?' His mother seemed to be fretting insistently already. Roop was her only source of comfort, after all.

'Don't be silly, Ma. Who's ever been injured by a cricket ball? We won't play with the hard ball that the older boys play with. Here, see for yourself. It doesn't hurt at all.' Roop's mother was still not convinced, but he began to play despite her misgivings. He could be as persuasive as his father was, and managed to coax the permission out of his mother.

Roop's grandfather had left behind vast quantities of land and property, so Roop's mother did not face too many difficulties in terms of daily existence. Most of the villagers were their sharecroppers. Her work was also made easier by their trusted house-staff member Hori Kai and his family, who did odd jobs for them.

'Sorola, Sorola! What are you doing? Where is Roop? Is he studying properly? His exams are starting soon.' Her elder brother's voice took her down memory lane.

Sorola. Apart from her husband, no one had ever called

her by this name. Her family had snapped ties with her long ago, when she had dared to marry someone from a lower caste. Her elder brother alone had not given up the relationship with his only sister. Her father, mother and sister-in-law would turn their backs whenever anyone mentioned her name in their presence. Her father-in-law's household had taught her how to be generous, how to fight.

Things would sometimes fall at night on the tin roof of their house, making a fearful din and scaring the boy. In winter, Roop's mother would comfort him by saying it was just dewdrops, but these lies did not work in summer. Sometimes, several stones would fall in succession on the roof, making the tin sheets clatter.

On some nights, someone would pound on the window of the room that opened into the lane behind. This made a racket too, and Roop would be frightened. So was she initially, but later grew accustomed to it. There had been no such sounds when Roop's father was alive, and Roop's mother understood their significance.

On her way to the toilet outside one night, she spied a dark silhouette near the bamboo grove in one corner of the courtyard. The beam from her torch was not strong enough, so she could not make out who it was. But she gleaned that it was a man. He shone his own torch on his exposed genitals. She raced back to shut the door, and panted for some time. Then she got into bed and pulled Roop's face into her breast. Roop slumbered on in oblivion.

The days after her marriage started to feel like an illusion, much like her own name. Those lust-infused rainy nights in ripe youth. She could have found ways to feed the flames of desire. Chances were abundant, and so were opportunists. That night onwards, even if Roop was deep in sleep, his mother would always wake him to accompany her outside. His sleep disrupted, he would get angry—all of which she understood. But he would not utter a single word to her. Gradually, he too began to understand.

Roop's mother slowly took on the appearance of a courtyard. Unlike the canopy over the areca nut grove, there was never ever going to be a safe haven over this particular courtyard. The devil's grass grew thickly, thick enough to keep the surface untouched either by rain or sunshine. Roop's mother kept him cocooned. He grew up, following in his grandfather's footsteps, or perhaps his father's.

Countless such nights made her transform herself into a frozen iceberg. She continued to bring Roop up.

A period of time rolled by.

Roop metamorphosed into a youth with a wide chest and sloping shoulders. The sounds on their roof had stopped by then.

'Sorola, your boy has got the second position in all of Assam. I am so happy today,' Roop's uncle shouted joyfully as he walked in through the gate.

'Second in all of Assam!' Sorola did not know how to respond. The courtyard filled with people within the hour. Her voice quivered as she answered a reporter's question, 'His father would have been so happy if he were here today.'

'Where are you planning to send Roop for his education now?' someone asked guilelessly, but the question left Roop's mother perplexed. It was true, his results were excellent, but there were no colleges in the neighbourhood suitable for him, which meant he would have to move away from the cocoon of her care. She recalled her husband's funeral for some reason. The courtyard had the same environment, the same crowd—but with completely different emotions. She had wailed that day when her world came crashing down—now her eyes flooded again in the same way. The fear of losing her son pressed down on her.

The day of Roop's departure drew closer.

'Ma, why are you worrying so much? I am not leaving for ever. I am just going to Guwahati . . . and I will call you regularly.'

'You wouldn't understand, my dear, how empty it feels when you are not here for even a couple of days. Now it will be for such a long time . . .'

Roop's uncle was becoming impatient for being made to wait.

'That's enough, Sorola. Let him go. He will miss the bus now.'

She hugged her son tightly. Roop stepped back from the embrace and, putting his hand on her forearm, said, 'Don't worry, Ma! Shyamali from Hori Kai's family will be staying with you from today. Don't worry!'

Roop got on the scooter, leaving his home behind. His mother watched him unblinkingly. Her eyes welled up, as did Roop's. Her sobs grew progressively louder. She had long ago lost the one person who could have put a hand on her shoulder and drawn her close to console her.

Leaving his mother drowning in a void, Roop left the house and the courtyard that she had nourished so carefully. For nearly a month after this, her heart wouldn't stop trembling, her soul wouldn't stop lamenting. She searched desperately for the boy who used to play cricket in the middle of the courtyard, the boy who would take the cows around along with Hori Kai while the paddy was being threshed, the boy who hated to see his widowed mother in white when the colours of her life ran out. Now it was he who had thrust her back into the same void and left for Guwahati. This had been inevitable, for he was too brilliant for the colleges in their vicinity.

She kept wondering . . . were her days of happiness going to prove so short-lived?

Though she had Hori Kai's youngest daughter, Shyamali, to keep her company at night, she would still start in her sleep and wake up several times. Sometimes she would get up in the middle of the night and, still muddled by sleep, rush to Roop's room. On other occasions she would lie awake and strain to hear faint sounds of distress from a corner of the courtyard. She was the devil's grass that had protected the courtyard after the deaths of her father-in-law and husband, but it seemed to have disappeared without warning. Earlier covered by devil's grass, the ground was now in search of a different sky.

Roop was home after his university examinations. The air was redolent with the heavenly fragrance of jasmine, kewra and orchids.

Hesitantly, he blurted out, 'There's a girl I like, Ma.'

His mother paused in the process of serving him lunch. An unspeakable fear, an unknown jealousy, gripped her heart. Ever since childhood, Roop had had no close friend besides his mother. He had always been open with her, but now, overcome by shyness, he could barely force out four or five sentences about the girl. The colours on his mother's face changed several times. At first, she felt a surge of anger and envy about this unknown girl. It was natural for her to feel this way about someone who was trying to snatch her son from her, the son she had brought up with such care.

But once Roop's mother had controlled these emotions, a new hope sprang up within her. She too had been on the lookout for a worthy wife for her eligible son. She had already been planning to tell him about Madhurima from the next village, when he came home for the Bihu festival.

Well then! Any girl who could lead a happy life with her son was good enough. It didn't matter if it was Madhurima or Nilima.

She was ecstatic, imagining a house filled with her son and daughter-in-law, granddaughters and grandsons. It was like she had spread an enormous mat in the courtyard. Sitting with her grandchildren on either side of her, she would unlock the treasure trove of stories that she used to tell Roop, stories that her grandmother had once told her.

Like the continuously shifting colours of monsoon, a variety of emotions flitted across her face until a soft smile appeared, at which Roop heaved a sigh of relief.

The touch of sadness and sorrow that had slowed time down was replaced now by cascading waves of happiness. There was a sudden burst of activity in the courtyard, for a new reason and occasion once again. Roop's mother beat her chest as she cried, this time in despair, at giving up her son from her bosom into the arms of her daughter-in-law.

Her daughter-in-law's name was Nilima. But Nilima did

not take her son away from her. Instead, Roop's mother gained a daughter of her own. Every corner of the house rang out with Nilima's sweet calls of 'Ma, ma . . .'

* * *

'Ma, it's getting colder now. Come inside from the balcony,' Nilima said solicitously. Her mother-in-law was ageing gradually.

Roop's mother's reminiscences ended here. Her collage of memories silently disappeared. It was close to the last chapter of her life when she had to leave the house and the courtyard behind. The courtyard in whose absence not a word of her story could be written.

She was very happy with her daughter-in-law. Nilima had been brought up with great affection by her parents. Roop's mother's first thought on hearing of her had been: 'A girl from Guwahati. What will she turn out to be like?' Roop was a straightforward, simple boy. Did he know how to select the right girl for himself?

'Girls from Guwahati are cunning. They use their beauty and bag of tricks to dupe simple and stupid boys out of their money. They do not even complete their education.' This was the substance of the women's gossip in the village.

Roop's mother saw Nilima in person for the first time only on the day of the wedding. There had been a few conversations on the phone before that. Though she had seen a photograph on Roop's mobile, a picture could hardly reveal the girl's nature.

But she was happy with the daughter-in-law she got. Nilima was efficient as well as diligent, and was more mature and understanding than her young husband. Roop's mother had just the one son, and she had lived her life holding him close to her bosom. What would happen to him when she was gone? When she bent to fill the pitcher at the well, her back ached. When she picked up the newspaper, she could not read the fine print. Her fears increased.

But Nilima put all her worries to rest from the very beginning. She couldn't have found a more capable wife for her son even if she had looked herself. The boy who used to skip along clutching the hem of her sador had grown so much that he was soon to become a father, but to her he was still the same small child.

She would watch television sometimes. One day, she saw a programme about an old age home. An elderly woman was recounting her life, speaking of her only son, whom she had raised by herself after her husband's death. She had ensured a good education for him, but now, after graduating from a reputed college and acquiring a good job, he appeared to have forgotten his mother. Apparently, he had married an unsuitable girl. He would call up his mother now and then, but his wife yelled at him if she found out.

This was similar to her story. She understood, from the unspoken words, the struggles that the woman had been through. Overcome by emotion as she told her story, the woman dabbed her eyes with the corner of her sador. The corner of Roop's mother's sador got wet too. But some of those were tears of relief, for Roop was not like this, and nor was the girl he had chosen.

She had no problems moving in with her son and daughter-in-law, she was happy to live with both of them.

But she was reluctant to leave behind the courtyard and the house, the courtyard that held memories of her husband and of her father-in-law.

She had dreamt of her father-in-law several times before leaving the house. As before, he was clearing the under-storey of the areca nut trees. She even dreamt of her husband after a long time. He didn't utter a word, standing in the middle of a large heap of rubbish with his back to her. He had always been a man of few words, though she had always understood what he meant. They had built their house bit by bit . . . how could they bear to see it abandoned now?

Roop's mother woke up fretfully after similar dreams on two successive nights.

She told her son and daughter-in-law, 'You can live there, I have no problems.'

Her refusal to move with them was obviously ignored. Both of them were concerned about her. Even a slight fever led them to call five or six times a day. They lived and worked far away. How was she to cope with the emptiness of the house all by herself?

She considered telling Roop about her dreams, but decided against it. 'Let things happen of their own accord this time,' she mused. And, finally, she left the courtyard behind without any arguments. Time's cruel deceptions dried up her tears.

* * *

'Roop, I can't bear to see the condition Ma is in anymore!' Nilima told Roop the moment he returned home from work. 'Apparently, she dreamt of both your father and your grandfather several times before moving. They told her not to abandon the house.'

'Oh! Things are getting serious then. I have to think of a way out quickly.' Roop's voice rose in panic. He didn't want to lose his mother.

'We should take her to Samiran tomorrow,' Roop declared after much thought.

'She's getting worse by the day. She sits in the balcony in a stupor and keeps gazing at the Brahmaputra in the distance.' Roop said in answer to his friend Samiran's query. Samiran was the best psychologist in town. Roop wasn't happy at disclosing these details. He went out of the doctor's chamber. Nilima could explain the rest better, she was closer to his mother nowadays.

Before going to the doctor, his mother had asked, 'I am all right. Why should I go to the doctor?' Nilima managed to take her along after much cajoling. She always listened to her daughter-in-law. Roop would be deeply troubled whenever anything went wrong with his mother. He rubbed his eyes on his shirt sleeve and went back inside the chamber.

Samiran had completed his enquiry. He said, 'Roop, she's feeling the absence of something that has had a deep impact on her life. This missing is making her behave unnaturally. The best course of treatment would be to fulfil this need.'

Roop arrived at a decision on his return from the doctor's chamber—he would take his mother back home.

'But what about our jobs? Have you thought about it?' Nilima asked.

'Now that the bridge has been built, we can commute

if required. It will take only an hour and a half by car. Of course, it won't be easy driving three hours every day, but we can take turns driving. Our problems are nothing in comparison to the sacrifices my mother had to make for me,' Roop said, gazing into the distance.

'Hmmm . . . I had the same thoughts. Don't worry about it being difficult, we will persevere as long as we can. And when we are away, we can ask Hori Kai's wife to look after her,' Nilima added in agreement.

The next Sunday, Roop's car stopped at the top of the driveway into the house. Hori Kai's grandchildren came running at the sound.

Roop's mother got out of the car unsteadily. Her eyes scanned every inch of the area, and then she took a deep breath.

Turning towards Roop, she said, 'We have to clean the grove. The courtyard too. We have to make it spotless. Your father will be angry if he sees it in this state.'

Nilima and Roop exchanged smiles. This fervour, this strength in her voice—how long had it been since they had last heard it? She had been forlorn ever since Roop's father had died. Now, being in the vicinity of the courtyard, she had found her husband again. Though fraught with impediments, her happiness suggested there was hope for improvement in her health.

Nilima's and Roop's smiles were faded in comparison to the bright sparkle in her eyes.

THE HUNT

Purobi Bormudoi
Translated by Mitra Phukan

A dying afternoon in late Aghon. There is a light mist in the December air. The trees have begun to shed their leaves. With their hands clasped tightly together, and their heads resting on their knees, the trees seem to be huddled up to ward off the chill. It is colder at Biswanath Chariali than it is in Guwahati. Here, the cold is a definite presence. It creeps silently through the many layers of warm clothing, and enters the body.

Sitting in the Maruti Gypsy driven by Rahim, an experienced chauffeur, three people are talking about the cold weather. They are Engineer Choudhury, Dr Saikia and their friend, Hazarika. Hazarika is the contemporary of Choudhury and Saikia, and their companion at card games. They had come from Guwahati to Biswanath Chariali yesterday. Amol, a relative of the doctor's, is accompanying them for the first time. He has recently joined service, and is distantly related to the doctor, being a nephew to him.

At this time, they are journeying towards Ahmed's house.

The vehicle is moving forward slowly. Both Hazarika and Choudhury know the location of Ahmed's house. In accordance with what has been planned beforehand, two youths have already been sent ahead to Ahmed's house. Ahmed is probably ready to receive them.

The two middle-aged men have come from Guwahati in order to hunt at the Pabhoi Reserved Forest. These days, they get bored rather easily. After amassing vast fortunes, and earning the respect of society, they sometimes feel a great sense of despair when they begin to think that they have completed their life's work. At times such as these, they feel weary of life. It is to escape this feeling that they sometimes come to hunt game. As kings and emperors of the past came out on royal hunts, so, too, do these men come out on hunting trips, in order to escape despair, weariness, a feeling of emptiness and the clamour within their hearts. They themselves cannot gauge whether they are relieved of these feelings of despair and of the clamour in their hearts after they return home from the hunt.

Biswanath Chariali is gradually turning into a small city. After crossing this small city, the vehicle enters a small rural path. Age has descended on the leaves of the trees lining both sides of the lane. The trees are beginning to shed their leaves. The dreary winter sky is visible through the bare branches of the leafless trees. The soft winter sun is slanting down the western sky. The van is moving forward on the twisty, unmetalled village road towards Ahmed's house. Every now and again, flocks of wild geese fly up, blocking the sky from view.

Amol, the doctor's distantly related nephew, had landed a job as soon as he had finished his studies. He is but a youth, as unformed as a tender cucumber. He has been intently observing the skies and the hazy, greyish villages. It is impossible to gauge his thoughts. The faces of the people sitting in front clearly reflect their feelings. Joy—the joy of the hunt. A kind of gravity has descended on their visages, like the kings and emperors of old and, like them, these men, too, are nonchalant and unconcerned. They are indifferent to a man ineffectually trying to ward off the chill with his woollen clothes by the side of the road.

The vehicle is going towards Ahmed's house. Ahmed is an expert shikari, a hunter. There is no other shikari to rival Ahmed in this region. The passionate hunters in the vehicle hire Ahmed whenever they come for a shikar here. Ahmed's domestic condition is not very satisfactory. He can barely support his wife and three children. He once had a bit of cultivable land, but it is not in his possession now. Ahmed's only income comes from hiring himself out as a shikari. Ahmed says that his wife and children do not approve of this mode of earning a living at all. But he is not fit for any other kind of work. He has, therefore, taken up this livelihood only because he has no other option. As soon as his son grows up and begins to earn, Ahmed will give up hunting and set up a small shop.

The vehicle moves forward slowly, and stops at the entrance to Ahmed's house. The men alight and sit on a bench on the veranda. Ahmed's wife comes out with a bota, a salver of areca nuts and betel leaves in her hands. Her face is crushed under some kind of mental strain. Ahmed, the shikari, comes out while the men are still chewing on the areca nuts.

Hardship and privation have put a stamp of sorrow on Ahmed's six-foot frame. He is slightly stooped. The veins stand out in his arms, the skin on his face is wrinkled, and more than half the hair on his head is white. Ahmed is wearing the baggy and rather soiled khaki outfit that is his costume while he is out hunting. On his feet is a pair of boots. In one hand he carries his gun, while a bandolier is strapped across his chest. There is not a single bullet in the bandolier.

The engineer, Choudhury, takes out the bullets from his pouch and slots them, one by one, into Ahmed's bandolier. For a while, Ahmed leans on the gun, as motionless as a statue carved from stone. The two youths who had been sent ahead to help with the arrangements have already carried hot cases containing parathas and chicken curry, as well as bottles of drinking water, into the vehicle.

All of them climb into the Gypsy. Ahmed's wife remains looking after the departing men with a pitiful look in her eyes. She has covered her head with the end of her sari. Her face is not clearly visible. But her eyes, glistening like those of a deer hiding in the forest, can be seen from quite some distance away.

Slowly, the wheels begin to turn. As the vehicle moves, it leaves behind its tracks on the dusty, unmetalled dirt road. Clouds of dust are churned up. The dust covers the leaves of the trees and the vegetation by the wayside in a thick layer. The vehicle crosses the small city of Biswanath Chariali once more. It is a bustling place, as busy and full of activity as a house where a wedding is taking place. The vehicle reaches the crossroads at Pabhoi, at the place where five roads meet. Rahim, the driver, comes to the back seat. Hazarika will drive the vehicle from this point onwards.

The Gypsy moves ahead on the winding lane that goes past the Dholi tea estate. There is an aroma of fresh tea leaves. The shade trees over the tea bushes are bare of leaves. The lane itself is damp. It had drizzled here a few days ago, and the lane still retains some of that moisture. The lane is topped with cinders. From afar, it looks like the black border on the sari of a young female tea-garden labourer. The aroma of the sweat of the toiling labourers mingles with the fragrance of the tea leaves. A few clumps of bamboo are scattered here and there by the side of the cindered track. The ground under these stands of bamboo is damper, for the shade has prevented the sun from falling on it. This late afternoon is preparing to curl up under a quilt. A rooster can be heard crowing from the labour lines. The setting sun waits just over the topmost branch of the bare trees. It will climb down in a short while, and reach the spot where the sky resembles an upturned bowl. Soon, birds will fly home and settle on these bare branches to raucously discuss the events of their day. The sky is ablaze with the glow of the setting sun, like a variegated canvas. It seems that a dexterous hand has just now painted the scene, with its setting sun, bare trees, tea bushes and the smoke-grey evening curled up in that December chill.

Gradually, the dust raised by the hooves of the flocks of homeward-bound cattle subsides. A few labourers warming themselves on small bonfires in front of their homes are visible. A couple of dogs are curled up near the warmth of the fires. The sun vanishes into the upended bowl of the sky. For a while, the light from the sun remains hanging on the leaves and branches. A little later, the light descends to the earth, and merges with it. Even as one watches, darkness possesses the path that snakes through the tea bushes.

The vehicle is new. It moves forward noiselessly. Ahmed begins to relate his hunting tales, as he has done on previous occasions, also. The others have heard them all several times before. They listen to him quietly this time too. This is Amol's first hunt. All this time, he has been looking out abstractedly at the world outside the vehicle's windows. Now, with the same abstractedness, he enters the world of Ahmed's hunting tale. Choudhury opens a bottle of liquor expertly, unhampered by the shaking of the vehicle. He pours out the drinks and the soda, and hands out the glasses to everybody sitting in the front seats. He then passes the half-empty bottle to those sitting at the back.

Glasses, bottles and packets of savouries begin to move up and down the length of the Gypsy at regular intervals. Hazarika, sitting in the driver's seat, steadily empties one glass after the other of alcohol, even as he drives on slowly. Amol is the youngest of the lot. In addition, he is, after all, also a nephew of some kind of the doctor's. He hesitates at first. But he is told that none of the usual rules or relationships are valid when out on a hunt. On a shikar, all family relationships, age constraints, education or money power become meaningless. All are equal. All are the same—hunters, shikaris.

The others sitting in the front and back of the vehicle are

all people who are in full control over both mind and body. Only Amol is of tender years. Gradually, he, too, begins to exert control over his mind and body. Gradually, he begins to lose his diffidence and inhibitions about drinking or smoking in front of his seniors. As soon as the inflammatory liquid burns into his belly, his mouth, too, begins to spout equally inflammatory speeches. Like the drab time of the day that wishes to curl up under the quilt, the dank thoughts in his mind vanish. He seems to come awake under the spell of some supernatural power. First, he begins to whistle a popular Hindi film tune. Later, he is heard singing the same song.

Outside, donning the garment of darkness, Nature waits motionless. At times, the music of the whistling wind outside can be heard over Amol's Hindi song. The trees are getting denser. The tea garden has been left far behind. The lights of the vehicle beam forth for a long distance through the shadows of the trees on the road ahead. The light of the headlamps and the shadows of the trees dance together deliriously in an endless line. The van moves forward at a slow and steady pace. The chiaroscuro of light and shade, too, moves forward. The play of light and shade looks like the madwoman who sits at the crossroads with her unkempt, matted and unmanageable locks. At other times, it resembles a serious, affectionate and loving patriarch. Occasionally, the aroma of damp earth and the odour of the forest permeate the atmosphere, adding enchantment to the damp winter evening. In the beam of the vehicle's lights, a few trees in the distance also resemble wise and holy sages immersed in deep and inviolable meditation.

It is quite dark when the Gypsy halts in front of the check gate at the entrance of the reserved forest. The light clumps together in the dense mist. A truck carrying timber waits in front of the gate. The truck driver is speaking in low tones with the gatekeeper. The gateman allows the truck to leave, and comes towards the Gypsy. Once more, words are murmured in low tones. Both the passengers in the car and the gateman know very well that the check gates at the entrances of reserved forests are there only to facilitate the entry and exit of timber smugglers and those who hunt wild game illegally.

After an understanding is reached at the gates, the van enters the unprotected reserved forest. The jungle becomes even denser from this point onwards. Sometimes, the vegetation encroaches upon the dirt track. The trees meet in a green canopy over the track. The ground beneath the trees is piled with the dead leaves of winter. There is a rustling sound as small animals, frightened by the sound of the vehicle and the beam of its headlights, flee over the dead leaves. Ahmed listens to the variety of rustling sounds, and, differentiating between the various kinds, says, 'This is a rabbit, this is a fawn, this is a leopard, this is a jackal, this a civet cat. Now this is the patter of the feet of a wild cat.'

Ahmed is a very experienced shikari. It is said that there is a tigress in this very jungle with which Ahmed is on familiar terms. Ahmed avers that he can recognise the sound of her footsteps even in the dark. She, too, recognises Ahmed's footsteps. She never harms him. Once the tigress, along with two of her cubs, was napping behind a bush by the side of the track. The cubs were playing with the tigress's twitching tail just as kittens frolic with their mother. One of Ahmed's companions had said, 'Shoot her between her eyes. . .' Ahmed had replied, 'She is a friend of mine, till today she has not caused me any difficulty. I warn you, don't shoot her, or else. . .' It was only after the tigress had left with her cubs, twitching her tail and glancing back at Ahmed, that the other men had breathed easily again. It seems that there is also an elephant here in the jungle that Ahmed knows very well. He steps aside whenever he sees Ahmed, leaving him free to move on.

The bottle has not yet been emptied. Ahmed is chattering nineteen to the dozen. Amol has stopped whistling Hindi film tunes and is listening intently to Ahmed's words. A thick cover of darkness has eclipsed the jungle. It is only possible to guess what is going on, or what creatures lurk, in the areas left untouched by the beams of the van. The two youths, Robin and Madhav, who are sitting near Amol, are quiet, though it is not really possible to know whether they are asleep, or merely silent. The stony banks of a small rivulet are visible in the light. The moon, which is today in its dark fortnight, is getting ready to appear in the skies. It looks as though the moon is trying very hard to break through the bank of fog. The vehicle stops near an enormous tree. The real journey will begin from this point.

The base of the tree is quite clean. Ahmed removes a few dead leaves and twigs from the ground, and sprinkles water from the nearby rivulet on it. He places a plantain leaf on the sanctified ground, and lights a packet of joss sticks. He removes the remnants of previously lit joss sticks, and leans the small axe, the machete, the hatchet, the guns and other weapons that he has brought with him, against the trunk of the tree. The boy named Madhav also places a bottle of liquor on the plantain leaf. Nobody ventures on a hunt without worshipping at this place in this manner. This is worship of the hunt, and of the goddess who is the presiding deity of this jungle. Questions of religion and caste do not arise in this worship at all.

After concluding the homage, all the men pile back into the van and open bottles of liquor. Even though Ahmed, too, is drinking, he keeps warning the others, especially the youths. Not much, merely, 'Just remember, you have come out on a hunt, don't cross the limits.' At Ahmed's warnings, the bottles and the glasses are put away.

Game is not usually sighted at dusk. Wild animals leave their lairs only at night. The foreign liquor has kindled the men's spirits. They are hungry, as well. Ahmed's wife is famed for her expertise in cooking. The mouth-watering aroma of hot parathas and chicken curry cooked with cashew nuts escapes the hot case and fills the interior of the car, announcing her culinary abilities.

After they have eaten, the men rest awhile. The group now becomes active and alert about the real purpose of this trip. A searchlight is connected to the van's battery. Ahmed reverentially closes his eyes and places his gun to his forehead. Only then does he hoist it onto his shoulders.

In the front seat of the Gypsy are Choudhury, Saikia, Hazarika and Rahim, the driver. Even though the space is cramped, they always sit in this manner. The hood of the car has been rolled back, leaving the top open. The two youths, Robin and Madhav, are entrusted with the responsibility of focusing the searchlight, alternately, with each other. Both stand up in the vehicle. Their hands are on the roof of the unhooded vehicle. One has the searchlight in one hand. Like an expert soldier, Ahmed stands between them. Amol has absolutely no experience of hunting; hence, he is not entrusted with any task. Today, his role is that of a spectator.

The vehicle moves forward. To Amol, it seems that it is moving at the slow pace of a heavily veiled young bride who is welcomed across the threshold of her new home by her mother-in-law. At this slow pace, the smoothly running engine of the Gypsy appears, to him, to have become absolutely silent. Robin and Madhav beam the searchlight on both sides of the track alternately. The powerful beams of the light penetrate the dense jungle. The light glistens on the dry leaves and the bare branches of the denuded trees. Drops of midnight dew hang from the branches. The light falls on the dewdrops, too, and is reflected back, creating a beautiful sight. Amol is looking with great absorption at this dark forest with its necklaces of dewdrops.

The moon of the dark fortnight climbs overhead, and lights up the land like a searchlight. They cross another part of the same rivulet that they had come upon previously. There is hardly any water here in winter. The vehicle crosses the ankle-high water quite easily. The radiance of the moon, and the beam of the searchlight creates ripples of light on the pebbles. A large flock of thousands of waterfowl can be seen in the beam of the lights as they sit on the trees by the bank of the river. The glistening black backs of the waterfowl reflect glorious prisms of light. For a single instant, the sound of the beating of waterfowls' wings is heard. The sound vanishes in an instant, and the flock sinks back into sleep once more.

The vehicle makes a low sound as it rumbles over the rocks strewn on the river bed. As soon as it crosses over, there is silence once more. The rivulet, calm in this dry season, is left behind. The waterfowl remain sleeping. The vehicle moves on towards even deeper forest after crossing the river.

Rahim, the dexterous driver, is now at the wheel. Ahmed, the skilled shikari, is sweeping the lighted area of the forest with alert eyes, on the lookout for game. Suddenly, Ahmed taps the hood with his hand. Hearing the signal, Rahim stops the car. As soon as the vehicle rolls to a halt, the lights are switched off. The forest is now lit up by the light of the moon overhead. Amol does not know who else has observed it—probably everybody has. But he thinks that only he has seen it. Pair of eyes glisten brightly in a part of the forest that the moonlight has not been able to penetrate. Unable to contain his excitement, he whispers, 'Eyes, eyes!' Ahmed scolds him roughly, 'Keep quiet!' Amol remains silent.

Once more, Ahmed taps on the rolled-back hood of the Gypsy. One should not utter any sound once game has been sighted. At this signal, Rahim moves the car slowly forward. Madhav aims the searchlight towards the pair of eyes. In the glare of the light, the eyes glow even more brightly. They stare unblinkingly. What are they looking at? What do they see? Do they see Death? Or do they see ambassadors who bring Death to those eyes?

Ahmed jumps silently out of the sluggishly moving vehicle. He moves slowly forward. Taking cover behind a tree, he raises his gun and takes aim at the centre of the pair of gleaming eyes. A heartrending scream is heard synchronously with the sound of the gun. The sound of something moving heavily into the distance, and then falling down, is heard. The beam of light follows the sound. Ahmed reaches the quarry. A huge deer is lying in a pool of blood. Its heart has spilled out of its body. Wildly, a life tries desperately to leave the body. Ahmed places the barrel of his gun on the body of the supine deer. Once more, there is a bang. A life leaves the body. Ahmed immediately cuts the veins on the deer's hind legs. There is nothing left for Ahmed to do after this. He returns to stand near the stationary vehicle. He lights up a cigarette, and begins to pace up and down.

Ahmed and Robin jump out as soon as the gun is put back into the Gypsy. The deer had not been able to escape very deep into the forest. Amol, too, gets down. All three of them stagger to the vehicle, dragging the deer behind them. The carcass is lifted into the back of the Gypsy.

The vehicle begins to move once more, this time, on its return journey. The faces of the hunt-loving passengers in the car are wreathed in victorious smiles. There is no reason now for them not to talk. The men sitting in the front and back of the vehicle begin to talk ceaselessly.

Ahmed's wife does not like him to hunt. Once, long ago, Ahmed had mistakenly fired at a pregnant doe. A fawn had been found inside the doe when it had been cut up. After this, Ahmed had not gone hunting for a very long time. As a result, his small son had succumbed to a slight fever, and died. Once, a headstrong youth had shot a suckling doe. A small fawn had died along with its mother. The fawn was roasted and eaten in the jungle itself. Ahmed's verdict: 'A tender fawn is not tasty.'

Rahim is not usually very loquacious. Now he, too, begins to narrate a story. A doe was washed down in the floods. She entered a village. The villagers gave chase to the doe, which entered another village. The people of the second village chased the first lot of people. A fight between the two groups of villagers ensued. In an effort to save herself, the doe entered a clump of bamboo. A small village boy killed her by hitting her with sticks.

Amidst the telling of these hunting tales, the vehicle reaches camp once more. The youths begin to skin the deer, and cut it up. The moon of the dark fortnight sinks into the western sky amidst revelry and laughter. The birds awake from their slumber. Dewdrops begin to fall from the leaves and branches of the trees. The forest is covered with a mantle of white fog. The sky and the river, too, awaken. A ripe wood-apple, the colour of freshly husked paddy, is seen hanging at the edge of the eastern sky.

In the morning, all of them wash themselves in the clear waters of the small rivulet. One of them collects dry twigs and boils water for tea on the bonfire. After eating biscuits and savouries, washed down with tea, the group returns to the vehicle once more. A packet of venison is kept aside for the gatekeeper.

Once more, the Gypsy moves forward. The group of people appears to be somewhat tired. After dropping Ahmed off, they will rest for a while at the Dak Bungalow. They will start for Guwahati only towards the late afternoon.

The men are sitting motionless in the Gypsy. Nobody

says anything. The huge deer is now only a lump of flesh. It is probably because of the sleepless night that he has spent, and his tiredness, that Amol begins to ramble unintelligibly. He wants to compare the deer's eyes with those of Ahmed's wife. Hers had glistened on her half-veiled face. The same pair of eyes. Lustrous, glistening eyes full of love and affection, pitiful eyes. Eyes that cowered with fear and insecurity. Yes, the same eyes, with the same glance, thought, language and the same yearning.

Amol has not slept at all through the night. Besides, it is for the first time that he has come on a hunt. He feels the pangs of grief in his breast. The hunter's aim has settled unerringly between the animal's eyes. No prey can escape the hunter after he has taken aim. Neither wild animals, nor Ahmed, the hunter, nor, indeed, any other person, can do so. Amol himself has not been able to do so. He is a prey to grief, poverty and sorrow, to disappointment and anger, to insecurity and betrayal. And, most of all, we are all prey to lovelessness and to cruelty. We cannot escape the hunter after he has taken aim. We are all going to morphe into lumps of flesh at some time or the other. Day by day, moment by moment, a desert is encroaching upon our hearts. A desert full of chaos and confusion. Everything is being captured by the arid sands. We are all prey to that arid desert within each one of us.

Amol looks back. Behind him, the dirt track disappears into the forest like a winding river. He presses his arms to his chest, as hard as he can. He will have to save his soul from the desert. Each one of us will have to save our souls. Yes, each one of us.

LAZY

Binu Das

Translated by Syeda Shaheen Jeenat Suhailey

Neena dragged the trolley out of the storeroom and rolled it into the bedroom in front of Arup.

In the evening she called Runi, who replied in a tone reminiscent of her father's, 'Do you think you can really go alone, Ma?'

'Let me see whether I can. I'm only going to Jiu's place. All of you worry too much.' They talked some more before Neena ended the call.

Runi was Neena's elder child, adored by Arup and Neena. She had gone to Delhi after school, getting a job there when she was done with college. She ended up falling in love with a colleague; the families talked, and then visited each other, finding nothing mutually unacceptable. The marriage was about to turn a year old. Four years younger than Runi, her brother Jiu was currently doing a film production course in Mumbai.

Arup was unhappy at this choice initially. 'Will this help

you support yourself in future? You really couldn't find some other subject to study?'

Neena had tried her best to make him understand. Eventually, giving his consent, he said, 'Do what you want, don't blame me later,' washing his hands of the matter and putting the responsibility on his wife.

'Are you sure you can go alone? You've never travelled on your own before,' Arup said to Neena, who was making tea in the kitchen.

'I think I can,' said Neena, pushing a cup of steaming tea towards Arup.

Arup brought up the subject again as they were having dinner that night. 'I don't believe you can go on your own. Think about it again carefully.'

Neena was reminded of Bondona suddenly, her roommate during their first year of higher secondary school. Once, when Bondona had arrived from her home in Sivasagar, one of the girls from the hostel asked: 'Did you come alone?'

'No, the bus had twenty-two other people.' The girl who asked the question was nonplussed at the response. The exchange circulated for days around the hostel.

Neena borrowed the answer now. 'I'm not going alone. The plane will have around a hundred or hundred and fifty people.'

Arup looked at her crossly and resumed eating.

That night, when he saw Neena packing her clothes, Arup said in annoyance, 'I'm saying this for your own good. Why do I even try telling you anything?' Turning away from her in a huff, he threw himself on the bed.

The next morning, he drove off to work without a word

to her. Watching the gate being closed behind him, she reflected, 'For my own good? Do you even have the time nowadays to think of what's good for me?'

Neena was often absent-minded at work these days. It was true she had never travelled alone. All the responsibilities and duties of the household had fallen on her after her marriage, leaving her with no time or opportunity for holidays or travelling. A full house, an unending stream of work. Not that she actually minded the work.

'Bou, I will have rotis,' her brother-in-law would order her lovingly as she was about to eat. She would rise to make them. There was no uniformity in each resident's dietary choices or mealtime.

Still, she tried to write in the intervals between her ceaseless chores. A short story was published in a magazine after six or seven months, and then a poem five months later. But, gradually, she could no longer make time even for this, and after Runi's birth, she was all but separated from the world of writing. On some days, she would feel sick and tired of all the housework.

'I hardly get the time for my own work,' Neena had confessed to Arup in the hope of some comfort.

'Your work? Is this not your work?' Arup turned the question on its head.

'Did I say that?' Neena retorted, surprised. And another Neena came to life within her.

Once, her friend Bobita had come over. Her husband Deepak was a former classmate of Arup's from the university. Conversations were in full swing that day. All of them went to watch a film and then ate at a restaurant. In the evening, the balcony was suffused in light-hearted banter. Arup would usually be asleep by the time Neena was done cleaning the kitchen, but that evening she looked at him out of the corner of her eye. She was glad to see her husband happy and enjoying himself. 'Neena, have you given up writing?' asked Bobita. 'I haven't seen anything you've written in a long time.'

Laughing, Neena answered, 'I hardly get any time after taking care of the children and their needs.'

Arup laughed as well, and said, 'You have to make the time if you want it enough. How will things work out if you're being lazy?' Neena felt Arup was slighting her. She may not have been a world-famous author, but she found comfort in putting her thoughts down on paper, or else they grew into thorns that pricked her. Bobita could see the sadness her eyes were trying to hide.

'That's all right,' Bobita intervened. 'The garden of stories will not wither away just because one woman stops creating them.'

Neena changed the subject quickly.

But thoughts of the work she wanted to do was lodged in her throat for quite a few days. Was she really lazy? How had she spent her time all these years, what had she achieved? All the labour she had put in from early morning till late at night every day—was it not work? The things she had done for such a long time, making a beautiful house and family— Arup had ground them to the dust in a single moment, with a single statement.

Did she even have the time to be lazy, she wondered. She was at work from the moment her eyes opened in the morning. Arup drank the cup of tea she made him before he sat down in the balcony to read the newspaper, while she woke up Runi and Jiu, made sure they ate and got them ready for school, after which Arup took them to the bus stop.

This storm was followed by preparations for Arup and her to leave for work. A part-time maid came by, staying at home till Neena returned. Runi and Jiu got home before their mother, so she also had to make their after-school snacks before she left. It was a similar situation as in the morning when she came back from work. She had to pick up after the children, keep the house in order, help them with their homework, decide what they would have with evening tea, what would be made for dinner—so much work.

She had to keep track of many things, but she had never complained about it. When it came to her household and children, she was happy to do everything that was necessary. Her children matured in front of her eyes. She didn't count how many seasons had passed—they flew by as fast as a winged arrow.

Runi was about to take her higher secondary final examination, and was rummaging in her mother's cupboard for something to wear to the farewell. She came upon a book half-hidden in one of the corners, a collection of short stories by her mother. There was a commotion as Runi called out to everyone.

'Papa, Ma, how come neither of you ever told us Ma writes?' she asked her parents sharply.

'I wrote these a long time ago. Give me the book, Runi.' Neena tried to take it away.

'I had this book published before you were born,' said Arup, looking at Runi with pride.

'She never seemed interested after that one book. Now she just idles away her time. She prefers the latest films and shows on Netflix and Amazon Prime to writing. Isn't that right, Neena?' Arup smiled at his wife.

Neena looked at him. How flippantly he had said what he had.

Once Runi found the dress she was looking for, she left the room with the cupboard doors still open, the book thrown carelessly on the bed. Arup went out of the room as well. Jiu looked into his mother's eyes. She had smiled at what his father had said, but Jiu came to learn that day how sad a smile could be. He sat down near his mother and stroked the cover of the book. Then he turned the pages one by one, flipping through the entire book attentively. It was as though a new chapter from his mother's life was suddenly visible to him.

'You wrote so beautifully, Ma, why don't you write nowadays?' said Jiu, holding the book out towards his mother.

'I keep thinking I will. But I don't seem to be able to write anymore.' Neena put the book back in its corner and closed the cupboard door. Giving her a hug, Jiu left the room.

Neena sat on the bed for some time, dazed. They had barely been married a year at the time. Arup had compiled all her stories, published in various newspapers and magazines, into a collection and sent it off to a press. She was so happy the day he had come home with the first copy of the book. Neena remembered that day very well even now. When and how had she slowly detached herself from that world she couldn't tell.

Arup knew these things well, and yet had spoken so thoughtlessly that it had shocked Neena. He noticed that she watched movies on Netflix, but what she did the rest of the time had not registered! This was the reason she felt she was drowning in a void even at the centre of a fulfilling family life and household. It was gradually becoming unclear to her what she really wanted to do, what would make her happy. The winds of despondency continued to overwhelm her.

Arup's dedication to his work led to promotions. As his responsibilities at the office increased, the time he could devote to his family decreased proportionately. Neena got busier too, taking care of everything that had to do with Runi and Jiu, who were quite grown up then. She found the time to relax only after both of them had gone away to study. The house felt emptier.

So, she picked up her pen and paper with renewed enthusiasm, but now she could not give form to her ideas. What had happened to her? Did she no longer know how to write after this long break? The blue pen lay with its cap in place on sheets of white paper not written on.

She confessed her despairing thoughts to Arup with great intensity. He replied nonchalantly, 'Why don't you write? Have I ever stopped you from doing anything? You have the time now, use it well.'

'Stop me?'

What was Arup saying? Had she ever done anything that would require Arup to stop her?

She was stunned. She was also hurt. How indifferently

he had answered. As though the mere desire to write would sow the fruitful seed of a new story. No need to till the fields at all. She found it hard to control the inner Neena's rage.

* * *

Once Runi was married, Neena began to feel lonely. Desolate times, really. Nothing could hold her attention, she didn't want to talk to anyone. Who was there to talk to anyway? Everyone had full and busy lives. Who was going to waste time on others? Neena tried to share her feelings of emptiness with Arup.

'Depression? How can you get depression when you have such a good life? Why do you keep thinking of these useless things? These are modern diseases,' said Arup, dismissing her complaint contemptuously.

She stood there dazed this time as well. If only instead of ignoring her he had said something like, 'Maybe try to write again, as much or as little as you want. Or do something you like. Your depression will melt.' But no, Arup made no attempt to understand.

Sometimes she did try to talk to Runi and Jiu. They gave her instructions as though they were the older ones.

'Start writing again, Ma.'

'Nothing flows from my pen,' she replied in distress.

'Write whatever comes to mind. Tear it up if you don't like it. But write anyway. We are not at home; you have plenty of free time now. Buy some good novels for inspiration.' They tried to boost a diffident Neena's confidence.

Jiu listened to her with great attention and affection,

but she didn't want to trouble him, since he hardly had any leisure hours.

And so, whenever she had a little time to spare, she opened a book and immersed herself wholly in the world of its characters. Still her hurt feelings gathered in her breast like cold ice. And a mountain of pride joined the glacier.

Sometimes Neena wondered whether she was indeed becoming lazy, as Arup insisted. Perhaps she should have learned how to make the time she wanted.

One day, she was talking with her colleague Rakhi Dutta, pouring out her heart to her. Rakhi was a well-known author who had joined Neena's school recently. A talented writer, Rakhi listened to Neena with warmth.

'Neena ba, I will also call you lazy. You will work twenty-four hours for your home every day but can't take out one hour for yourself? And you say you are a writer?'

She encouraged Neena to write again.

Neena retrieved her old diary from the cupboard after many years. She cleaned the diary, whose cover had now faded. Perhaps this was the one place where the tally of what she had received from life, and what she hadn't, was maintained. Clutching it, she went back a long way in her head, rubbing away films of dust to uncover the memories of all the places where she had been. These she knitted into a story, which she sent off to *Jonaki* newspaper, whose Sunday section featured poems and stories.

After this, she made sure to check the paper every Sunday. No, her story hadn't been published yet. She had written it after such a long gap, maybe it did not match their standards.

There were so many good writers now. She concentrated on her housework.

'Neena, a story of yours has been published,' Arup shouted from the table where he was drinking his tea and reading the newspaper.

'Give it to me, let me see.' Neena snatched the paper from his hand and went into the bedroom.

'Congratulations! Let me read it,' said Arup, following Neena into the room.

Glancing through the story quickly, she passed the newspaper back to Arup and immediately called up Rakhi.

'My story came out today, Rakhi. How will I ever thank you?' Neena's voice trembled with emotion.

'No need for thanks, Ba. Just give me a treat one of these days,' Rakhi answered happily.

Neena's heart felt full. All her hard work had borne fruit. Many people she knew rang her through the day to convey their good wishes after reading her story.

* * *

'Ma, I have some good news for you,' Jiu told Neena during a call late at night.

'What news, Jiu?' Neena asked eagerly.

'That creative writing workshop in Mumbai I had told you about is coming up again. Two weeks. You must join this time.'

Oh! Neena's son had brought her such hopeful news.

Neena's heart swelled. She had no idea that such workshops existed, and in Assamese at that. Neena immediately told Jiu that she wanted to join, and asked him to get all the necessary information.

'I want to, very much. But what will your father say?'

'I will manage him, don't worry.'

She sent her biodata as Jiu had asked.

* * *

Taking courage from Jiu, Neena let Arup know of her plans. Arup's reaction was typical of him—'Creative writing workshop? Is this something another person can teach you? Write whatever you want at home. You've never been anywhere alone. Do you think it's easy to go to Mumbai by yourself?'

This time Arup's words were not enough to vanquish her will. She primed the inner Neena, who had been searching for the moonlight all along, to step out on the bright path that Jiu had laid out for her.

For the first time, Neena was to go to her son's place by herself. He was supposed to show a new world to his mother. She took a month's leave from her school. She did not tell Arup about her plan to stay in Mumbai for almost an entire month, for then he would not only have stopped her from going, but also rebuke Jiu harshly.

Arup travelled a lot for work. She had managed everything on her own when he was away. So why wouldn't she be able to manage herself now? Shutting the now-full suitcase, she fetched another, smaller, one from the storeroom.

* * *

Arup dropped her at the airport and advised her repeatedly on what she should and should not do. A barrage of advice.

'I've been alone for a long time. You don't need to worry now.' With these words, Neena walked into the airport.

Arup looked at her retreating figure till he could not see her anymore. She let out a sigh of relief when she sat down in the plane. She felt as though she were ready to fly away for the first time in her life. Jiu had booked her a window seat. She looked at the distant sky, lit brightly by the sun, but with a few challenging clouds hanging in it.

VALUES

Mamoni Raisom Goswami
Translated by Gayatri Bhattacharyya

Pitambor, the merchant, sat dejectedly in front of his house. He had still not taken off his mud-plastered shoes. Indeed, he had a weakness for his pair of old leather shoes . . . At one time, Pitambor had been a fit and well-built man. Now he was about sixty years old and although that was not an age that could be said to be 'old' for a man, all kinds of worries and discontentment weighed him down, and these had taken their toll on him. His face sagged and he had a haggard look about him. His head was always downcast; he could never look directly at the person he was talking to. The way his head invariably hung down, it seemed as though he was scrutinising the ground, searching intently for something.

A big teak tree had recently been cut down, and Pitambor sat on the stump looking at the children with their improvised fishing rods, trying their luck in the gutters that lined both sides of the road. The incessant rains of the last few days had made the entire village muddy and slushy. The sides of the dirt road had become covered with all kinds of vegetation, both edible and useless, and the frogs were having a great time jumping from one ditch to the other.

Pitambor was looking intently at one particular boy who was trying to untangle his fishing line from an arum plant, when a deep voice suddenly caught his attention. He looked up to see the priest, Krishnakanta, standing near him. 'Pitambor,' said the priest, 'you have been sitting there engrossed in looking at those children for a long time. You were sitting exactly like this when I passed by some time ago, and you are still sitting in the same place in exactly the same way, staring intently, and with a peculiar longing, at those children. Is it because you do not have any children of your own? "Whose beloved child is being chased to the waters? Call out and bring him back so that I can kiss him!" —Is that what you are thinking? By the way, is your wife any better? Is she able to leave her bed and do some work now?'

'No. How can she move about when her hands and feet have become swollen? I have already taken her to the hospital in Guwahati at least twenty times, but she is no better.'

'There seems to be no chance of you ever having any children of your own then? So your family will become extinct,' said the mischievous and malicious priest.

Pitambor sighed in dejection. What else could he do?

Krishnakanta stood there silently for a while. He was dressed in a knee-length old dhoti, a tattered and worn-out warm kurta, and an equally old 'endi sador'. His cheeks were hollowed as he had only two front teeth left—all the others had fallen—so that when he spoke, his face took on an odd and twisted shape. His eyes had a malicious and sly glint, and his balding pate only intensified his cunning look. He came near Pitambor and whispered, 'Have you given any thought to what you will do if something happens to your wife? Have you thought about marrying again?'

Pitambor was about to answer when he happened to look up, and his eyes fell on Damayanti. She was the widow of the priest, Shambhu, who had died not too long ago. Everyone knew that she was a woman of loose character, and after her husband died, she had become the centre of attraction for all the young men of the village.

Krishnakanta called out to her, 'Where are you coming from, Damayanti?' he asked.

'Where do you think I am coming from?' she replied. 'Don't you see the 'endi' silk worms in my hands?'

'So you have started hobnobbing with that Marwari businessman, have you?'

Damayanti did not reply and, instead, started to squeeze out the water from the bottom end of her sopping-wet mekhela. As she bent down to do so, her blouse rode up to her breast, exposing her slim, soft, and fair waist. Neither man could resist looking at this attractive spectacle, but the priest quickly averted his gaze. After she had squeezed out the water, she calmly walked away, without even bothering to look towards the two men.

'They say that she has no inhibitions and even eats fish and meat,' said Pitambor. 'Yes, I heard that too,' replied Krishnakanta. 'She has put all the Brahmins to shame. She does and eats whatever she likes, and does not care for any traditions or rules. In the beginning, after Shambhu died, when she cooked fish for her two daughters, she used to go down to the river and bathe and then cook separately for herself. But now, I am told, she does not bother and even sits with the girls and eats the fish.'

'Yes,' replied Pitambor. 'I have seen her taking fish from the fishmonger woman in exchange for paddy.'

'Dear me!' exclaimed Krishnakanta. 'What is the world coming to! A widow buying fish in exchange for a bit of paddy!

'Softly, Purohit, softly,' said Pitambor. 'You do not need to publicise the fact that a Brahmin widow is eating fish. Such things are common these days, even in orthodox places like Dakhinpaar and Uttarpaar. And I do not really think it is such a sin. These old rules should be abolished.'

Staring at the departing figure of Damayanti for some time, Pitambor asked, 'Bapu, what is the condition of your clients these days? Has it changed at all?'

'What a surprising question, Pitambor! You know everything and yet pretend not to know! Don't you know that it is because of the quarrel between my brother and myself over our clients that I am in this poverty-stricken condition?'

'It is mainly because your brother went around telling everyone that you do not know how to read Sanskrit,' replied Pitambor.

Krishnakanta jumped up in anger. 'Tell me,' he shouted, 'how many priests are there these days who can recite the mantras as clearly and correctly as Narahari Bhagabati? He and I studied at the tol, the school for priests, together. He was the one who got the caning, not me. No, no. The main reason for our poverty-stricken condition is the attitude of the clients—of those people who ask us to go and conduct their pujas for them. We priests who know how to conduct the rituals and pujas should not have been in such an impoverished condition. In the olden days, there was no problem getting at least one sacred thread, a pair of dhotis and some money from each of our clients every month. But nowadays everything is different. People want to perform the rites and pujas, but are unwilling to pay the priests. Only the other day, one of our oldest clients, Mahikanta Sarma's two sons, were taken to Kamakhya temple for their 'upanayan', the sacred thread ceremony. One of my clients in Maisanpur, Surja Sarma, held the shraddha ceremonies of his mother and father together on the same day. People are gradually starting to ignore the Nandimukh shraddha, the shraddha ceremony of nine ancestors which is such an essential part of the wedding ceremony. And, of course, the smaller rituals and pujas, like the naming ceremony, house-blessing puja—Basanti puja, purifying a house by holding a 'hom', organising a purifying and sanctifying holy fire if a vulture happened to roost on the house . . . these have become things of the past. Time was when a man had to undergo a purifying ritual if he lost his sacred thread. But how many Brahmin boys today even chant the Gayatri mantra!'

Pitambor had been listening to the priest's lecture without saying a word. His mind was still on Damayanti, and her lovely, silky-smooth back exposed when she bent down to squeeze the water from her soaking-wet mekhela. He thought that he had never seen such a beautiful woman's waist or back before. And it was not as though he had not seen or touched a woman's body before. He had married his second wife just two months after his first wife had died, mainly because his first wife had died childless. But this second wife was a sick woman. Soon, she became almost completely bedridden due to acute rheumatism. Pitambor had taken her to doctors in Guwahati many times, but to no avail. Ultimately, the woman had become thin, more like a skeleton than a living woman. She lay in her bed all day, quietly watching her husband's behaviour. The man seemed to have almost lost his mind, longing for a son to carry on his family name. People said that he was waiting impatiently for his sick wife to die. After a few years, he had given up going to the hospitals in Guwahati, and had given up all hope for a son and heir. The priest was now in front of him lamenting his lot in life, but Pitambor hardly heard him. His wife had signaled to one of the servants from her bed, to go and give a 'mora', a cane stool, for the priest to sit on, but Pitambor was not even aware of when the servant had come and gone!

'You are so absentminded, thinking all the time only of the fact that you don't have a son and heir, that many people here in our satra have started saying that you are becoming unbalanced, that you are on the verge of insanity,' said Krishnakanta, referring to the religious and cultural institution. 'There are hundreds of people in the world who do not have children. It is nothing so terrible. And why don't you think of what our gurus have said—that families, sons and so on are, after all, transitory things, and hence valueless—simply manifestations of "maya".'

Pitambor simply lowered his head in dejection. The priest noticed that his hair was greying, that his eyes were circled with small cobweb-like wrinkles. The man had become completely unmindful of how he dressed and his shoes were caked with layers of mud.

Krishnakanta was overwhelmed by a sense of pity and compassion for Pitambor. Just a few years ago, the older citizens had called him the 'gora soldier'. He was so well-built, fair and fit. There was no dearth of money or means, but the poor man had no peace of mind. His granary was full, but there was no one to enjoy it.

Suddenly, Krishnakanta said something almost unheard of! But before saying it, he looked all round to verify that there was no one nearby. But the door of Pitambor's bedroom was wide open, and he could see the skeletal body of Pitambor's wife lying on the bed. Her sharp eyes, he noticed, were shining with a peculiar brightness—as though she was trying to find out what the priest was saying to her husband. Krishnakanta was shocked to see that a single glance, even from a distance, could be so keen, and could express such heartfelt sadness. Even so, he whispered to Pitambor, 'If you think that you can help me with some money, I too will help you to get what you so desire.'

'How?' asked Pitambor. 'How will you arrange things?'

'Don't worry about the arrangements. There will be no problems,' said the priest.

'What do you mean?' Pitambor was curious at this point.

'What I mean is that I will arrange matters so that when you meet her, there will be no question of her not conceiving. I have found out that she has aborted and buried the results of her illicit and guilty pregnancies four times!' Krishnakanta said with confidence.

Pitambor almost shouted, 'Bapu, are you talking about Damayanti?'

'Yes, yes. I am talking about Damayanti,' replied the priest. 'Our Brahmin girls have started going across the Dhaneswari river to marry Sudra boys. Don't you know that the Gosain of Mukteswar Satra's son has gone and married a Muslim girl? It seems that our Gandhi Maharaj has shown this path—that caste and community do not matter. That is why I am thinking about this matter of Damayanti for you.'

Pitambor jumped up in excitement. 'What matter are you talking about?'

'If you so desire, you can make Damayanti your own woman.' Krishnakanta glanced towards the open bedroom door again. The eyes of the woman lying on the bed were wide open and it seemed as though they were burning with a fierce fire. She was staring at Krishnakanta.

Pitambor ran and tried to clutch the priest's hands, but the latter hastily stepped away. He had just bathed and was on his way to the Adhikaar's house. He had been asked to bathe the image of Murulidhar in the Adhikaar's temple, because the regular priest there had gone to Guwahati. It was a very important duty and he had to be clean and untouched by any other person, particularly one who was not a Brahmin. But the priest's words had opened an unthinkable world for Pitambor and he did not know how to thank the man.

'So Pitambor,' said Krishnakanta, 'It seems that you have been thinking about this for some time.'

A happy smile played over Pitambor's lips. Once again,

Krishnakanta glanced towards the bedroom. The woman's eyes were now shut, but it seemed as though she was undergoing some terrible suffering and pain. Touching the priest's feet, Pitambor spoke humbly and pleaded, 'Bapu, do this for me. Everyone knows that she goes out at night to bury the things she aborts. I know it too. But she is a Brahmin woman and I am a Sudra. If she comes to me, I will place her on a pedestal and worship her.'

A sly and crooked smile spread across Krishnakanta's toothless mouth. 'It will not be easy. I will have to negotiate, I will have to get the two girls to agree to it, and for that I will have to bribe them with sweets from your shop.'

Pitambor got up hurriedly and went inside. The eyes of the woman lying on the bed flew open. She had probably just shut her eyes and was not asleep. She saw her husband go to the small, wooden box that was placed on top of a stool, and open it; she also saw him going out to Krishnakanta again after a while.

'You will let me know everything soon, won't you?' he said to the priest.

Taking the twenty rupees from the Mahajan, the wily priest went away with a mischievous smile . . .

Seven days passed without any word from Krishnakanta, while Pitambor waited eagerly every day for him. He had seen Damayanti a number of times; making her way to and from the Adhikaar's house to deliver the sacred threads she spun from the finest cotton. It was only now that he looked at her properly and discovered that he had never seen a woman as beautiful as her.

Her mother, they said, was from the village of Routa

situated on the banks of the Dhanasri river. After seeing Damayanti now, Pitambor came to the conclusion that the Brahmin girls from near the Dhanasri river must be among the most beautiful women in the whole country. Her father, the priest Purnananda, had once lost a couple of his ploughing bullocks, and at that time he had had many clients in comparatively distant places like Maisanpur, Gargora and so on. Searching for his precious bullocks, Purnanada had gone to the village of Routa on the Dhanasri river side. No one seemed to know why he had to go so far to find his cows. But it was then that he saw and married the beautiful daughter of Bhagawati of Routa village. No priest of the area had ever before married a girl from so far away. . .

It was the month of June, and the rivers and wetlands were overflowing with water. Both sides of the dirt road were full of shrubs and climbing plants that invariably came with the season. The road running in front of Pitambor's house was now covered with mud and slush. But, in spite of the muddy and slippery road, Pitambor saw Damayanti walking along, plucking the edible greens such as the tasty 'kolmou' or water spinach which grew in abundance on the roadsides in the wet weather. She had lifted her mekhela up to her knees, and was accompanied by her six-year-old daughter, who was completely naked. Damayanti's legs and hands were soft and shiny, and healthy, like a new mango plant. Her hair which cascaded down her back was a reddish bronze colour, very much like the colour of rusted cannons, he thought. Oh, yes, the exact tinge of an old, rusted, iron cannon! Pitambor remembered the huge iron cannon that was found when they were digging a well. It was said that the Burmese soldiers had left it behind when they had to retreat. He remembered that a group of students had come after some time and hauled it away.

After looking at her for a while, Pitambor plucked up the courage to speak to her. 'You will get sick if you walk about in this foul weather, in this dirty, muddy road,' he said. She turned and looked at him, her face and eyes expressing a surprised curiosity. But as earlier, she did not utter a word in reply. 'If you had only asked me I would have sent my servant to get you all . . .' But before he could complete his sentence, she turned to look back at him again. Pitambor felt as if her eyes that were blazing with a fiery look would burn him to ashes.

Without wasting any more time there, he walked rapidly away and sat down on his usual seat on the stump of the teak tree. He glanced towards his house and saw that his wife had taken to her bed again. She had tried to get up that morning after a long time. Her wasted limbs creaked with a ghastly sound when she tried to lift herself up, and she felt dizzy, so that she had to go back to her bed again. Now she lay there staring at her husband coming and going. Pitambor gazed at her with a cruel, and at the same time, somewhat embarrassed look. It was time for him to go and give her one of her medicines, and he was quite aware of it. But he did not get up—he simply sat where he was, looking down, contemplating his shoes. There were only four people in their satra who wore shoes—the clerk of the satra office, the two sons of the Adhikaar and he himself. He bent down and tried to clean his mud-caked shoes with his handkerchief, and then again looked up at the road to see if Krishnakanta had come. But there was still no sign of him. As he sat waiting impatiently, a bullock cart came creaking into his compound. It was his tenant farmers bringing his share of the paddy they cultivated. On any other day, Pitambor would have rushed in enthusiastically and counted the baskets of paddy. But today, seeing that his master was absentminded and indifferent, the servant came and counted the baskets and stored them inside the granary himself. After some time, having rested and partaken of some refreshments, the tenant farmers came as usual and took their leave from Pitambor. Also, as usual, they had some complaints about Pitambor's tight-fisted attitude. But nothing moved him today; he sat where he was, silent and indifferent.

Looking inside, he saw that his wife was lying with her eyes open. He noticed that someone had replaced a tumbler of water near her, and he remembered that the time for her medicine was past. But he got up anyway and was about to go and give it to her when he heard Krishnakanta's voice. Forgetting about his wife's medicine, he quickly put on his shoes once again and hurried to the gateway where the priest was waiting for him.

His wife's eyes, he noticed, seemed to be unusually weak—the fire that normally gleamed in her eyes whenever she looked towards him, seemed to be slowly dying out.

'Mahajan,' the priest called out.

'Yes, Bapu. Tell me, have you any news?' asked Pitambor.

'You will have to go to meet her on the coming full moon night in the dhekal, the room containing the dheki,' he said, referring to the wooden pedal for cleaning and pounding rice. 'It's located behind her house.' The priest looked furtively all around, and continued. 'I have found out that she is not pregnant at the moment. Her daughter told me this after I had bribed her with sweets. It seems that it is not yet a month since she terminated her last pregnancy. The girl is too young to understand these things. It seems that she had helped her mother by holding an oil lamp while the woman finished her job. She also told me that this time her mother had used a spade belonging to a Brahmin boy from Chataraguri. This boy used to come cycling from his home to study in the college near here. He is a boy from a well-to-do family, but of loose character. He came, and instead of going to college, he hid his books inside a basket of rice in Damayanti's hut and spent his time with her. He used to spend the money for his college fees buying things for Damayanti. The foetus she buried this time was this Brahmin boy's . . .'

'Listen Mahajan,' the priest continued, 'I have spoken to her about you. At first she was quite angry, "That Sudra man", she said. "How dare he even think about such a thing! Does he not know that I am the daughter of a good Brahmin priest?" I replied that everyone knew that she was a Brahmin woman. But now that she had taken the sinful path, there could be no difference between castes. I also told her that no Brahmin would stoop to marry her now. They would simply exploit her body and then cast her aside like the useless husks of the sugarcane stalks. I told her that you would marry her with all due rituals, as soon as your ailing wife died, that your wife is even now as good as dead. After you marry her, she would live a good and prosperous life, I told her. Do you know, Mahajan, when she heard all this, she went into her hut and cried her heart out, I do not understand why . . . She came out after some time, wiping her tears and said, "I do not keep well these days, and it would be a relief if I could lean on someone's shoulders." I replied that it was not surprising that she did not feel well, after having aborted no less than five or six times within a short time; that if her case happened to come up in a Panchayat meeting, no one would even consider going near her, because anyone found to be giving her even a tumbler of water would be fined a sum of twenty rupees!'

"'What other option did I have?" she wept. "My daughters were starving. The Adhikaar's wife used to ask me to do small jobs for her in the kitchen. But now she says that I am not fit to work in her kitchen, that whatever I touch will become impure and contaminated. Before I used to be asked to spin and make the sacred threads, the 'laguns'. But now the Brahmin families of this area will not allow me to make the 'laguns'. They say that I am corrupted. The tenant farmers know that I am all alone with no one to look after me or my interests. So they too have started behaving like monsters. What do they care that I am a lonely Brahmin widow with two small daughters? How can I fight them? I own some acres of farm land in Satpakhila, but I have not been given my share of five maunds of paddy ever since my husband died. I have not been able to pay the revenue tax for that land for three years, and the land could be auctioned off any day now. What was I to do? I had to think of feeding my two daughters . . .'"

But, in the meantime, Pitambor was getting more and more impatient. He almost yelled, 'Yes, yes, I understand all that. But what about me, my case?'

'Yes, I am coming to that,' replied the sly priest.

'She said, "He is a Sudra belonging to the fourth caste. Having relations with him . . ."' But finally she told me that she would meet you on the full moon night in the dhekal behind her house.

Pitambor could hardly contain his joy. And, taking advantage of that Krishnakanta said, 'But you will have to give me about one hundred rupees. Damayanti says that she needs a mosquito net, and the two girls will have to be given sweets from Bhola's shop.'

Pitambor hurried inside and went towards the small wooden chest he kept in a corner of the room. His wife opened her sick eyes and followed his every move. Suddenly, he shouted at her, 'What are you staring at? One day I will come and pluck your eyes out!'

Krishnakanta sat outside listening and understood what was happening inside the bedroom. He was a sly fox. When Pitambor came out and handed him one hundred rupees, he whispered, 'If necessary, give your wife a small pill of opium that night. She lies on that bed listening to everything, and understands everything. It is better to be careful.' And laughing meaningfully, the sly Brahmin priest took his leave. The woman on her bed simply shut her eyes.

Krishnakanta walked back a few steps and said, 'Damayanti is very keen on money. She acts like a tigress where money is concerned . . . Never mind, you will be able to hold her hands intimately.'

The Mahajan felt rather guilty, and looked back at his wife. But no, she had heard nothing. She was asleep. But her dry forehead glistened with perspiration.

It was the full moon night of the monsoon month of Ashaar. Pitambor wore an endi kurta and a fine Santipuri dhoti. Across his shoulders he had thrown a sador of fine cotton. After a long time today he brought out the mirror with the wooden frame and scrutinised his face. He had shaved that morning, and now out in the sunlight, he could see fine wrinkles covering his face, and he was somewhat disturbed. It seemed to him that the wrinkles were a net and he was the fish trapped in the net of his wrinkles.

In due time, he walked towards Damayanti's house. It was located near the bridge on the Singra river, beyond the forest of teak trees. Very few people of the satra lived here, and it occurred to Pitambor that Damayanti was able to live as she did only because she lived in an almost-deserted area.

He looked up to see some mushroom-coloured clouds floating in the sky, looking, for the entire world, like cannons. And that round moon! As though it was deer shorn of its skin. As though someone had come and wrapped her dotted skin around the cannons. A skinned deer—her meat shaking uncontrollably without the skin to bind them in place! Lovely fresh vigorous meat! This skinned deer suddenly transformed into Damayanti. A completely nude Damayanti! There were her lovely breasts—like a pregnant goat's stomach. Her body was the colour of tender bamboo stalks, and her lips? They were soft and lovely like freshly cut mangoes oozing sweet nectar . . . Pitambor could not stand there any longer looking up at the sky, weaving fantasies about the woman. It was deathly quiet and completely deserted. It was the night of the annual 'bhaona' performance, and the entire village had gone to see it. Indeed, she had purposely chosen this night!

He heard some jackals howling from the thorny shrubs nearby, and he walked rapidly to Damayanti's hut. He took off his shoes and sat on the plinth. A heady fragrance of the Champa flower floated out from somewhere. Damayanti lay with her younger daughter on a small cot set between the basket meant to store rice and a dome of ripe jackfruit. The girl was drowsily writing the letters of the alphabet on a slate with a dirty, old lamp with a broken chimney as the only source of light. Leaning against the wall, Damayanti was watching the man. After a while, she beckoned to him to come inside, and sit on a 'mora', that was placed nearby. A small earthen lamp filled to the brim with mustard oil, burned nearby. For some reason Pitambor was afraid to look at her body in the pale light of the lamp—he had a peculiar feeling that everything might be over if he did . . . It was all a land of illusion, he felt. Was this Brahmin widow in front of him a real woman?

'Have you brought any money with you?' Pitambor was startled into reality. He had not expected her first question to be so very materialistic.

'Whatever I have is yours,' he replied and handed her a cotton bag. She took the small bag and put it inside a cane basket that was hanging on one of the posts of her 'dheki ghar'. In the meantime, the girl who was writing the alphabet went and lay down with her sister and instantly fell asleep. There was a very low cot in one of the rooms that was used to store the baskets of rice. Damayanyi's husband, who had been a priest, had been given those baskets during the shraddha of the Adhikaar's brother.

Pitambor followed Damayanti and sat down on that cot. After a while, she came to him . . .

Two months passed by. One day, after the Mahajan had left her, Krishnakanta happened to see Damayanti bathing in the river, and made fun of her, 'Why Damayanti, I never saw you coming to the river to bathe after you spent the nights with the Brahmin boys of Dudhnoi Bongora!'

Damayanti did not reply. But the sly priest was not put off. 'I suppose it is because this one is a sudra?'

Again she did not reply, but she suddenly jumped up and, going to a corner, she began to vomit violently.

For some moments, the priest stood where he was, dumbfounded. Then he said, 'This must be Pitambor Mahajan's child then?'

Again she was silent. But Krishnakanta continued, 'That is very good news. The poor Pitambor will be very happy, he was almost going mad at not having any children! Then I will go and give him the good news.' After a pause he said, 'Listen, you must not worry or feel bad. Our Gandhi Maharaj did not believe in all this business of caste. He said that all men are equal and the same. Just you wait and see, Pitambor will marry you with all the proper rituals as soon as his wife is dead. I am sure that you are aware that the villagers were getting fed up with your way of life, and were thinking of having a Panchayat meeting about it. I don't think you know that some time back one of the things you aborted and buried beneath the clump of bamboos was dragged out by a jackal and deposited in one of the priest's courtyards. And have you any idea how much that poor man had to spend to get himself purified—and for no fault of his own!'

Damayanti started vomiting again.

'Be careful, Damayanti,' warned Krishnakanta. 'Do not do anything this time. Even after knowing all about you and your repeated abortions, Pitambor is willing to accept you. If you do anything this time to damage the child within you, I tell you, you will go straight to hell. No one and nothing can save you.'

And Krishnakanta went to give the Mahajan the best news he had ever heard. 'Pitambor, if she does not go and abort this child, you can be sure that she will not be unwilling to marry you.'

As usual, Pitambor was sitting on the stump of his favourite tree. He had not even bothered to take off his mud-caked shoes. Hearing the priest's words he started trembling in sheer excitement. He would be a father! Can it be true? Would he really be a father at long last? But of course it must be true. The Brahmin priest himself had told him so.

He stood up, deeply agitated, and started walking about aimlessly.

Krishnakanta said, 'What is the matter with you! Why are you walking up and down like a monkey! But of course you have more than enough reason to be happy and excited! It is not a small matter to become a father after thirty years of waiting! A very great fortune indeed!'

Suddenly, Pitambor came and knelt down in front of the other man. 'Bapu,' he pleaded, 'please see that she does nothing to frustrate the dearest desire of my life. You well know what kind of men my father and grandfather were. Only a sufferer can understand the despair of a childless man! Besides, she is a Brahmin woman from a priest's family and now she holds my life in her hands! What will I do, Bapu, what will I do?'

Krishnakanta lifted one hand as if in blessing and said, 'I will keep track of her and what she does, like a vulture keeping track of a corpse. Do not worry. I will also warn the old woman who helps in these dreadful things. But I will need some money to bribe her too.'

This time Pitambor did not have to go to his small box to get the money. That morning he had sold all the fruits from his seven jackfruit trees, and the proceeds were still in his pocket. He took out the entire bundle of notes and handed it to the priest. Extremely pleased at the way his plans were going, Krishnakanta put his hands on Pitambor's head and blessed him.

Now when Pitambor went to the bedroom, his eyes fell straight on his sick wife's eyes. And, in spite of himself, their sad and desolate expression moved him to compassion. But the next moment, he regained his composure and forced himself to anger. 'Hey, you sick and barren woman! How dare you stare at me like that?' And he yelled out to his servants, 'Come, come! Lift this bed. Take it to the small room next to the dheki room. Come, hurry up!'

No sooner said than done! Along with four of his servants, Pitambor carried the bed with his wife still lying on it, and put it inside a small, dark room without any sort of ventilation, near the room where the paddy and the dheki were placed.

Since his affair with Damayanti, Pitambor seemed to have almost forgotten that his wife needed at least some looking after, and had to be given medicines regularly. She was just skin and bones now, and seeing that their master did not bother about her, the servants too had started to neglect her. They were even careless about bringing her food on time, and often did not bother to bring her a glass of water with her meals let alone give her the required medicines on time. The poor woman's throat would often become parched and dry with thirst, but she would not utter a word of protest. People said that she looked more like a corpse than a living woman. Even now, when her husband brought her to this small, dark room and left her there, she kept quiet. But, surprisingly, even in the dank darkness, her eyes shone brightly, and it seemed as though she saw, and understood, everything that was going on, more clearly than if she was out in the open.

The very thought of fathering a child made Pitambor delirious with joy. He lived in a world of joyful imaginings—the child in Damayanti's womb seemed to him to be already a boy, then a young man. In Pitambor's imagination, the boy walked along the banks of the Dhanasri river, holding his father's hands! The ever joyous and sparkling golden thread that binds fathers to sons seemed to stretch happily far into the distant horizon, where all was sheer happiness, where the ties and traditions of family were an unbroken saga of joy . . .

Pitambor got a couple of his trusted servants to bring down an old wooden box from its perch near the roof of his room. When he was sure that he was alone, he opened the box and took out a bundle tied in an old gamosa. In the bundle were a few pieces of half-burnt bones, the 'ashthi' of his long dead father, and entwined in the dried-up bones was a chain of the precious poal or coral beads that were so much a part of the traditions of Assam. Pitambor remembered how, as his father lay on his deathbed, almost choking with the effort to speak, had said, 'Keep this chain of my poal beads carefully. Your son will wear it, and then his son, and then his son's son, and so on. It will be the living symbol, the everlasting flag of our clan . . .' The old man died before he could complete the sentence. Pitambor took out this chain now, then wrapped the pieces of 'ashthi' in the gamosa again, and put the bundle back in the old box. Finally, he called in his servants and had the box put back in its old place on the shelf.

Days passed into weeks, and weeks into months, and Pitambor became more and more impatient to hear some news. He had heard that a foetus that was five months old could not be aborted and he calculated that it was now three months since she had conceived. As he waited, each day without any news, it seemed to become more and more unbearable. Each passing day loomed in front of him like a mountain he had to cross in order to gain access to his happiness and survive.

Almost every moment he seemed to hear the Brahmin woman's footsteps approaching him, and he imagined that she was whispering to him, 'Mahajan, hurry up and prepare for the wedding rituals. I can no longer hide my condition. Do you not see how big my stomach is? Hurry up. Get the wedding preparations ready.' Again, 'All those things about Brahmins and Sudras, about Hindus and Muslims, are just a lot of nonsense. We are all human beings, and you will find that the same red blood flows inside all of us . . . Get the rituals for the wedding ready.'

She seemed to walk with ghungroos tied to her feet and she came to him with tinkling feet. He imagined her lovely fair and slim legs . . . 'Mahajan,' she seemed to whisper, 'nowadays I do not bother to go and bathe in the river after I sleep with you. Go, get ready for our wedding . . .'

Three months passed by uneventfully, and the Mahajan still dreamt of walking along the Dhanasri river banks with his hands on the shoulders of a handsome youth—his son!

It was the late monsoon month of Bhadra and often violent storms lashed the villages. A storm had been steadily gaining momentum since that afternoon. Going inside to shut the door of his wife's room, he noticed that her eyes today burned more brightly, more malevolently than usual. They looked to him like a shining snake that passed by him in the dead of night. As the storm raged, the lamps were blown out, and all other sounds were drowned out by its sheer ferocity. Pitambor shouted for his servants, but no one could hear him. The only sounds to be heard were the rumblings and thundering of the storm and of trees being felled, either being struck by lightning, or being blown down by fierce winds.

There, another tree had crashed down! Which tree was it, Pitambor wondered. Somewhere in the distance, he saw a streak of lightning that had definitely struck another tree! He could hear the frightening sounds of the tree being split down the middle and crashing to the ground. He went outside to see which tree had fallen and what disaster this terrifying storm had caused.

In a corner of the grounds, the fruits of seven of his coconut trees had been heaped up waiting to be sold. Now he saw his servants running about trying to salvage them and store them inside the dheki ghar. Some of the fruits which were still on the trees thudded on to the ground, being blown down by the wind. No one could hear anyone else . . . But gradually the storm began to calm, the rumblings and thunder died down, and a heavy rain lashed the village. Lighting the lantern again, Pitambor could now see the heavy raindrops, but he could still hear the tinkling sounds of Damayanti's anklets as her feet came towards him . . .

Suddenly, amidst the rain, Pitambor heard someone calling him by name. Picking up the lantern, he hurried outside and saw the priest coming towards him, completely drenched and shivering. Pitambor was frightened. Only some extreme news could have prompted the man to come out in this terrible weather. Krishnakanta held an umbrella over his head, but it had so many holes that it afforded no protection whatsoever. His dhoti had been drawn up to his knees, and only a thin 'sador' that was dripping wet, covered his bare body.

Holding up the lantern Pitambor shouted out, 'Bapu! What brings you out in this foul weather, so late in the night?'

Somehow, Krishnakanta managed to come and sit down on the plinth of the house. Leaning the torn umbrella against a post, he took off his 'sador' and tried to wring it dry, and wiped his wet face with it. Then, pointing a shaking finger at Pitambor he said in a choking voice, 'Pitambor, when your first wife died, there were three inauspicious stars in the ascendant, three puhkars. Three or four?'

'I do not remember,' replied the Mahajan. 'Why?'

'When three puhkars are found at the time of death of a person in the house, even the dubari grass dries up and dies. When your first wife died, there were three puhkars. And, as a result, the ill effects are still there. Everything is dead and gone!'

'What has happened, Bapu? What is wrong?'

'She has destroyed it, Mahajan, she has aborted! She refused to carry the seed of a Sudra man! She belongs to the highest Brahmin clan, a woman from the Sandilya gotra! She has spoiled your seed, Pitambor, she has finished off her pregnancy!'

(The youth holding Pitambor's hands let go and fell into the depths of the Dhanasri river. Who was it who had fallen? Was it Pitambor, or the young man? Dear God, who was it that tumbled and fell headlong into the deep waters of the river!)

One day soon after this, Damayanti heard a sound near her house in the dead of the night. Someone was digging something beneath the clump of bamboos behind her dhekhal. She shouted, 'Who is it? Who is there?' and woke her elder daughter. The six-year-old girl and her mother stood near the window, listening. The sounds of digging came from the same place where the two of them had gone in the dead of night two days ago and buried that thing the woman had ruined. Mother and daughter had gone out that night and dug a hole with the spade the Brahmin boy from Chataraguri had given them. The young girl had quivered in fright when she heard the jackals howling nearby. And today, the unmistakable sound of digging came from that very same place. Thud, thud! Thump, thump! Standing near the window, the two of them saw a lantern burning in the spot, and in the light of the lantern they saw the figure of a man, a strong, well-built man digging away at the very spot where Damayanti had dug just two days ago. Indeed, he was digging up the same hole!

Damayanti's entire body and soul trembled at the sight. The man was Pitambor Mahajan. He had hung his lantern on a bamboo, and was digging fervently at the spot. The man had assumed a terrifying aspect and he was hacking at the earth like a mad man. She trembled in fear and terror. Should she shout? Yes, of course, she must. Such a terrible thing was happening in her own house—of course she must shout!

'Mahajan! Mahajan!' she shouted. But there was absolutely no response. He simply kept on digging.

'Mahajan, why are you digging up my ground?'

Pitambor looked up towards the window, but did not utter a word.

Damayanti went almost wild with agitation. 'Yes, I buried it. But what will you find there now? It was just an unformed lump of flesh.'

Pitambor lifted his head and looked at her. 'It was my child! I will at least feel the flesh of my flesh! I will feel my child, my son and heir, with my own two hands!'

A WAGTAIL'S SONG

Bikash Dihingia
Translated by Harsita Hiya

Do we find every answer we seek?

Is life all about solving questions without answers, or finding questions for the answers we already have? The beauty of a garden is said to fade once the wilting flowers are plucked out. Is this what happens to the pleasures of life when we bury the past in favour of the present?

Closing both my diary and my eyes, I leaned back in my chair. The ceiling fan whirred overhead, giving rise to a faint melody. My study lamp rested on the desk, gazing down at the open diary as though trying to read its pages. The only other light in the tiny room was a dim blue bulb staring at me. A cluster of fireflies had flown in though the open window as I sat there, lighting up the nooks and corners of the room.

My exams were coming up, the pressure rising day by day.

College in the mornings. Tuitions in the evenings. Assignments at night. After dinner, I would study until about 1 or 2 a.m. so I could wake up sharp at 6 the next day to tackle the same routine. A few moments around midnight accounted for all the personal time I had in a day. Every night, after the clock struck 12, I took out my diary, pouring into its pages all the thoughts that had been badgering me during the day.

I owned these minutes. They were mine alone. Even though I never let a day go by without opening my diary, I wasn't always able to find something to put in it. I was often seized by despair and emptiness, by messy thoughts and unhappy images, when I sat down to write.

At times like this, I yearned for a cigarette, so that I could release all my troubling thoughts with the smoke, but I couldn't summon the mental strength to light one. I wanted to bawl my heart out too, but I couldn't do that either.

I was a boy, you see, and boys didn't cry.

I was a good boy, and good boys avoided bad habits and rude language.

I was a model boy, in fact—and model boys respected their elders and heeded their parents.

'There's another you within you. A you chained up inside your mind. That is the you I see and feel.'

The Silkori was flowing quietly in front of us. Wagtails were prancing around on the grassy bank, dancing and burying their noses in the sand. We were sitting together in silence that afternoon beneath the hollong trees, watching the water flow past. That was when he had spoken up, interrupting the stillness.

For the longest time, his words kept ringing in my ears. Another me within?

What a strange claim! How was it possible that there was another me buried within? And how could someone else feel his presence even before I could?

I knew he had far greater knowledge and a better understanding of things than I did. I was unfortunately not as worldly. I had never learnt to be, nor found ways to seek such experience.

The wagtails looked on as he laid his head on my lap and closed his eyes, his nostrils flaring with every breath.

Emotions never felt before awakened in my heart.

'I will have to go away after the annual exams,' I whispered hesitantly to him—to my best friend Surya Deep—running my fingers through his hair.

In a flash, he grabbed my hand and placed it over his chest.

'Where?' he asked, looking up at me from my lap.

His heartbeats travelled through my palm, becoming one with my own pounding heart. I couldn't understand what his eyes wanted to tell me then. I didn't realise what he had said without saying.

'My father has opted for a transfer to Guwahati,' I answered. I couldn't keep looking at him. I saw him tearing up. It was as if he wanted those tears to lead him to me—so that he could swim across the salty stream into my eyes and travel downwards to make his home in a corner of my heart.

Lost in his eyes, I became a stranger to myself as I uttered those words—all because of that unfamiliar sensation stirring within.

A boat suddenly came into view near the opposite bank of the Silkori. Someone was out fishing in the river.

How badly I wanted to embrace Surya, but how could I? Boys weren't supposed to hug boys. Boys weren't supposed to be attracted to boys either. I recoiled from myself in fear.

Was I not a boy then? The other side of me he was talking about—was he like Pallav, our classmate? I couldn't understand why my chest felt so heavy, why I was suddenly so ill at ease.

Pallav had been bullied by everyone in our class. The boys called him Maiki and Leddis, taunting him for his 'effeminate' ways. Changing his name to the feminine version, some of them had even christened him 'Pallavi'. It was no surprise that he preferred the company of the girls, often bursting into tears around them.

I am not like him at all. I am normal, just like every other boy, there is no other me hiding within, I assured myself.

Back then, almost every classmate knew how close Surya and I were as friends. One would get mopey whenever the other was absent—practically all the teachers knew this as well.

Ours being a higher secondary school, there was a large number of students. So much so that it was impossible for all of us in class eight to fit into a single classroom. So, we were divided into three sections. Surya was in Section C at first, but, in that particular year, the teachers transferred him to mine, Section B. I barely knew him before that. He had been no more than another classmate, our interactions limited to saying hello to each other, to thumps on the back while passing each other in the hallway.

One day in class, I excused myself and went out for a drink of water. It was the science period for Section C. Surya was sitting absentmindedly, staring out of the window into the corridor. Walking past him, I noticed he had a smaller book concealed within his science textbook. Feeling a pair of eyes looking at him, Surya scrambled to hide the book in embarrassment. He must have thought a teacher had spotted him. When he saw me, however, he abandoned his efforts and, squinting at me, covered his mouth to stifle his giggles.

I felt an odd sort of joy at that moment. It was the first time I had felt that way for someone. The first time I had known attraction towards another person.

What was the book? I wondered. Why had he chosen to read it instead of paying attention to his lessons?

How desperate I was to talk to Surya!

Did his parents love him the same way as mine, I wanted to ask him. Did they too make him kneel in the courtyard for hiding other books inside his textbooks? Did he lie about things? Did he know how to swim? All these questions, and many more.

It didn't take us long to become best friends after his transfer to Section B. We often jumped over the school wall during recess in those days to sneak off to the river bank. Sitting by the coolly flowing Silkori, he told me stories from all the books he had read, while I coached him for the things he was unable to understand in class. He taught me how to sky-gaze, climb trees and float in the river, while I . . .

Actually, I couldn't teach him anything meaningful.

'I don't miss home when I am with you,' he would often tell me before parting.

Away from the monotonous life my parents had forced upon me, Surya Deep opened up a wide, new world to me.

In the moments spent with him, I forgot all the warnings and rules laid down by my parents. Their worries about me faded too, alongside the memories of every caning.

Unfortunately, the two of us were caught one day. As a reward for skipping school, our principal called up our parents and made it a point to tell us off in front of the entire assembly of students. It was the first time I saw grief clouding my father's eyes. Upsetting my parents left me in great turmoil. I wanted to weep my heart out, but no matter how agonising it was, I didn't allow myself to cry.

'Oi, are you a maiki? Crying over the smallest things! Can't we have a little fun with you? Leddis, salla!'

That was how everyone would tease Pallav. He was given these names the day he had burst into tears on being teased. No, I could not let myself break down.

Away from prying eyes, I felt Surya squeezing my hand.

At home, my mother made me kneel down in the courtyard. I did as I was told without a word of protest.

'What has come over you?' she kept asking me, 'Why did you go to the river with that boy? Didn't you stop to think what would become of us if something happened to you?'

I had no answers. I remained kneeling with my head bent, staring at the ground as I counted the strokes of the cane on my back. Surprisingly, I felt no tears welling up. Perhaps, I had already become as impervious as a stone.

From my early childhood, my parents had brought me up with a great deal of love, but also with an extremely firm hand. My father had given my mother free rein to discipline me however she saw fit. My grandparents and other relatives were strictly forbidden from interfering in the matter, for such attempts had always led to arguments in the household.

The years went by and I grew older, but my parents continued treating me like a child. They still dictated all my likes and dislikes. Everyday, they reminded me of the sacrifices and hardships they had endured for my sake. Against every dream of mine they pitted at least a dozen things they had been forced to give up on my account. I had learnt by now that I was nothing more than the fruit of their labour. The sole aim of my existence was to realise their unfulfilled dreams.

'There's another you within you.' Surya's words echoed in my head.

That afternoon, we had made our first and last visit to the river after getting caught. Our annual examinations were looming, they were barely a week ahead.

I was furious with him. Perhaps because he wanted to introduce me to the one I had kept hidden. The side of me I wasn't yet ready to meet.

'We are done talking with each other from now on,' I told him and walked back home, never looking back.

We were so young then.

Despite being the same age as me, Surya knew more of the world. He was far better with feelings too. His mind was freer, more open than mine. I had always envied him for this, even if unconsciously.

But the envy turned into fury that afternoon. After all, he had discovered my hidden self before I had. I could have anticipated it. But Surya, like his name, was the sun itself. A shining star unable to conceal his light.

'Who, are you running from, me or yourself?' he had cried out from behind me, watching me walk away.

My anger grew even more, engulfing me.

* * *

Guwahati wasn't an entirely unfamiliar place. I had accompanied my mother to this concrete jungle many times during the holidays to visit her brother—my maama—who lived in the city with his family. When my father chose to take a transfer to Guwahati from Bokulbari, it was my maama who helped our family buy a small piece of land in the city. The construction of our new home began immediately afterwards.

Oh, to think of the many dreams I had to leave behind in Bokulbari! Plans for a long stay at my dear friend's home after our examinations, plans to go around the neighbourhood during Bihu singing together, plans to look for baby parrots in the forest on the opposite bank of the Silkori . . .

But my parents had already made up their minds.

Despite giving up her own home for my father, Ma had never liked living in Bokulbari. I knew this well enough. The conservative society in the village had kept my progressive mother from dressing and behaving the way she wanted. All the same, she had borne it all for the sake of my father, who dearly loved the place where he had been born and brought up.

But, concerned deeply about my education, Ma had often made sharp remarks to my father during our final days in Bokulbari.

'He has to get into a good school before his matriculation examinations. Here he will only slip out of control . . .'

Unsurprisingly, there wasn't any 'good school' nearby which could meet my mother's expectations.

Then there were my maama's calls, adding to the pressure.

'He will have to take his matric exams in two years! How will he get good marks if he stays put in that village of yours? Send him to us. We'll get him admitted here, and—'

But there was no question of my mother letting me live on my own. And as for my father . . .

At last, after much deliberation, the decision was made. My father set about making arrangements for his transfer, proving once again how much he loved me.

For the sake of my future alone, he left his home in Bokulbari to settle elsewhere. The list of everything my parents had forsaken for me had now grown heavier.

The new chapter of my life in the glitzy city began as I started in class nine in an expensive and reputed Guwahati school.

How odd, how peculiar city life was!

My classmates welcomed me by teasing me and calling me a gaonliya—a country bumpkin. They also taught me how to swear. Everyday I would learn from them a treasure trove of strange new curses.

'Oi! Stay away from Xopun. He is gay.' Two of my new classmates-cum-self-proclaimed-well-wishers told me once. Still far too immersed in my past, I wasn't yet spending time with anyone new. Xopun had merely tried to be friendly.

'Gay? What does that mean?'

The boys burst out laughing. I had sealed my own reputation as a gaonliya.

'It means he likes boys!'

Their explanation gave me goosepimples. The afternoons spent with Surya by the river began spinning around in my head.

But I wasn't ready to be another Xopun, so I took it upon myself to emulate the other boys—to never be teased or bullied or considered a laughing stock.

I grew more and more wayward by the day. I abused things I never intended to touch. Devoured films I never intended to watch. I was drawn to every forbidden thing. I fought hard against myself to turn into my peers. Simultaneously, I carried on another fight within, trying my best to become the son my parents wanted me to be.

It was all so tiring at times. Lonely too. I missed Surya constantly, longing to leave everything behind and sit beside him by the river.

It had taken me too long to realise that he was the only one who truly knew me. That day on the river bank, he had been trying to help me prepare for war. A war I hadn't seen coming at the time.

I slowly tried to do away with his memories after leaving Bokulbari.

I never went back to our old home after moving away. I fell in love several times in those days (or pretended to?) I did everything I could. I relished the forbidden joys of youth, and yet, I never felt happy. Not truly.

Even during the most intimate moments with my lovers, Surya's flared nostrils kept flashing before my eyes. The soft curves of a girl against my ribs only reminded me of the way Surya's chest heaved with every breath. I failed to stick to any of my lovers. They kept leaving me one after the other.

I couldn't find anyone else to share the restlessness inside. It wasn't like I didn't try, but there was hardly anything more I could do without risking my reputation and becoming the butt of everyone's jokes. What I wanted most of all was to lead a normal life.

In trying to find someone who understood me, someone who could fill my heart with light, I faced one disappointment after the other. I was desperate to meet Surya. I missed him so much.

Him. Bokulbari. The Silkori. The prancing wagtails.

The more I tried to forget them all, the stronger the memories became over time.

I even tried to stalk him on social media, but he was nowhere to be found.

'Is he even alive?'

A hidden desire to be reunited with him kept all such thoughts at bay. How is he, I wanted to know, how does he spend his days without me?

And yet, I was hesitant to ask any of my acquaintances about Surya. (My attempt, I suppose, at what they call sulking.)

Does he not think of me at all, I wondered, not even once?

I busied myself working to fulfil my parents' dreams. After all, they had sacrificed everything for me. I was the only one they loved; this was why I didn't even have siblings.

To calm down, I started writing in my diary. By now, I was aware that I had begun harbouring resentment towards my parents. I no longer loved them as much as I was supposed to. Yet, I couldn't deny that they had my best interests at heart. They were only tough on me because they loved me.

'I have grown up, Ma.' I often wanted to scream, 'I know the difference between good and bad. I know which paths to take and which to avoid. Let me breathe freely, Deuta. Let me think for myself. Let me choose!'

My screams remained black letters scribbled across the diary's pages.

'Ma, I am only straying further, you know? Deuta, I no longer feel attached to the two of you. I know this is a bad thing, but I just can't seem to love you anymore, no matter how hard I try. And yet, I cannot protest—you gave birth to me. Gave up so much for my sake! I have to do my part and give back. I have to return what I owe you. I cannot upset you at any cost.'

The lock screen of my phone lit up, accompanied by a slight vibration, showing me a notification.

It took me a while to weather the storm raging inside and anchor myself to the present.

'Surya Deep sent you a friend request.'

The unexpected words shook me to the core. Thump-thump-thump . . . my heart was hammering away.

I went to his profile. A nameless hope had walked into my life after such a long time, filling me with happiness. I could barely wait to see my dear friend for the first time after five long years.

But his page rekindled all my indecision. The sight of him in his profile picture, smiling next to a girl, instantly triggered a pang in my heart.

This was the kind of feeling which had kept me from loving myself, kept me from being comfortable with who I was.

Now I could feel something stopping me from accepting the request.

Why? Why did this keep happening to me? Why did these feelings I was so desperate to deny keep forcing me to be attracted to Surya?

Was this what they called love?

I sat up in shock.

No, I couldn't let this happen. My parents would lose face. What would my classmates say? And the girls who had left me? I did not want to be a rumour travelling from ear to ear. I did not want to be a topic of ridicule and gossip.

I shut the window, closed my diary and turned off the light. At last, I fell back on my bed.

'That is the you I know and feel.' A young Surya's voice reverberated in my ears.

The Silkori looked swollen. Rows of crepe-myrtle blossoms stood swaying on its banks as Surya held me in his arms beneath the hollong trees. One of the dancing wagtails came to perch upon his shoulder. Our breaths mingled. His sweaty nose brushed against my nostrils. A boat made its way to us across the Silkori. With a smile, Surya took the hand of the girl who had rowed up on the boat. Crepe-myrtle petals filled the river. I kept looking at the two of them from under the tree. The river flowed on as I stood and stared. They went down the purple water, eventually disappearing in the distance.

A vacuum engulfed my heart. The wagtail came to sit on my shoulder. A scream rose, wanting to escape my chest.

At that moment, I was finally awoken with a shudder. I

now had even more questions for Surya, the one who had haunted my dreams until sunrise.

Did he too yearn for me as I did for him?

How was he? Where had he been all these years? Did he ever think of me in the days we were apart?

'You have a new message request.'

My phone buzzed with a new notification the moment I turned on my data. I tapped it quickly.

The message was from Surya.

'Why do leaves fall when they ripen?

Why does sorrow in partings reside?

Why are the banks still while the river glides?'

Once again I had no answers, only a hundred questions wriggling in my head. My pride turned to vapour all at once. I quickly accepted the request and began typing a reply.

'Surya . . .'

By now, the sun had emerged smiling, disturbing the sleep of the concrete jungle.

I stood up and opened the window towards the east. A million rays of the sun, of Surya, rushed in to caress my face.

THE BURIED POND

Niruja Bora

Translated by Rashmi Baruah

'There is no fish in the pukhuri, my dear.'

Her grandmother's words had filled her young impressionable mind with puzzlement. A pond without fish! And such dirty water! No one seemed to clear the abundant water hyacinth or the leaves that had fallen into it. Maama's house also had a pukhuri . . . but that one had a lot of fish. Her maternal grandmother used to say it was good to have a pukhuri in the backyard. She herself has seen the huge fish they used to catch there; her uncle would send them over to their house sometimes.

Her father would have thrashed her if she were to ask anyone about the pukhuri. It was only when she went into the backyard with her grandmother that she pondered on the idea of the joiyal pukhuri. Why did people say it was joiyal? Was the pond really haunted? Sometimes, sitting idly at the study table, reading the news or when her attention wandered when trying to study, she would find her mind filling up with random thoughts about the pukhuri. She would absentmindedly read a couple of chapters out loud, and then, suddenly, on hearing someone's voice, abruptly come back to the present and look around to check whether anyone had noticed her daydreaming.

Sometimes, when she played kabaddi with her friends in the fields, they used to talk of the ponds in their backyards. She would then pipe up, 'We have a pukhuri too.'

'But a pukhuri without fish . . . ha ha ha . . .' her friend Mamoni had burst out laughing. Not having a clue about what Mamoni was referring to, the others had continued talking about their own pukhuris. She had rolled her eyes at her friend, who tried to stifle her laughter with a hand over her mouth.

When her paternal aunts—the three older jethais and two younger pehis—came home, they would all sit out in the yard exchanging news and stories about the village. Whose daughter had got engaged, whose son had joined the army, which elderly people died, who had had a baby . . . their chats were lively and never-ending. Even as she played with her cousins, she would eavesdrop on their conversations. Maybe there was some important news that she had missed out on. Sometimes they would whisper in one other's ears, but she would still manage to overhear those. The subjects disturbed her during her studies. Her mother would sometimes say, 'Gaat letha lagil . . . bhal khobor dei'. But what was this? Letha meant a problem, didn't it? The woman had some physical problem. Then why would they say it was good news? Thoughts like these plagued her when she sat down to study.

But no one ever spoke of the pukhuri. Nor did she dare ask anyone. In any case, she went about her day without speaking much. Even her curiosity about many things could not make her utter a word. She saw her father scold her mother for the smallest of things and make her cry. A fear for her father grew within her. It did not escape her eyes when her mother wiped her tears in the darkest of corners. Being the eldest among the siblings, everything probably touched her heart more than it did anyone else's. She had three younger sisters. Some say that was the cause of her father's sadness—that he had sired four daughters but no son. At the same time, expecting her mother to love her seemed a task as impossible as reaching up to touch the sky. Taking care of the three younger ones meant she did not have any love left over for the eldest one. It was perhaps this feeling of neglect that made her thoughts about the joiyal pukhuri resurface every once in a while.

There had to be a reason it was described as joiyal. The moment anyone stepped near it, someone or the other would yell, 'Don't even look at the pukhuri!' The trees drooping towards its water made it look even more gloomy and frightening; it gave her goosepimples.

Her grandmother, bent though she was from the waist, would grow spices like amomum and turmeric by the pukhuri. And sometimes, she would break off a tiny stem of the amomum and bring it for them to eat. She would accompany this with a warning, though. 'Eat this only if an elder in the family brings it for you. Make sure you never go near the pukhuri alone.'

As she grew older, she began associating the word

'joiyal' with the pukhuri. And she also began to understand her father's harshness better. When her uncle's wife gave birth to a son, the happiness and celebrations in the family knew no bounds. But now she began to feel her mother was gradually being made to feel redundant. She could see the household responsibilities being increasingly thrust on her mother, even as her father neglected his wife. And while she ruminated about these questions, she noticed her mother too suppressing her own thoughts and immersing herself in housework.

'Xoru buwari has saved the family line from dying out,' she overheard some old lady from the village whispering in her grandmother's ears. She realised that not giving birth to a son was being spoken of as the 'mistake' that was 'being corrected'. Though she seethed inside, she remained silent, as always.

'The family line can be saved even after giving birth to four daughters, your mother-in-law is a living proof of that. She went on to become the mother of eight children eventually,' she heard someone from the village telling her mother. Like many other things, this too made her pensive. Her father was born after three elder sisters and not four. And after him came two more sisters and a brother. That made a total of seven, not eight. So why had the lady talked of eight children? Now she had one more thing to worry about on her desk. By now she had learnt how to keep on writing even while mulling over things. She needed answers to the questions bothering her . . . she finally made up her mind to ask someone.

She had never seen her grandfather, who had died before

she was born. Did he get angry as often as her father did? Did he neglect her aunts for being girls? Did he yell at her grandmother for even the smallest of things? Her questions grew until they collectively seemed to have reached the size of a big bundle. But she found no answers to any of them. She had to find explanations to certain questions, for they were slowly beginning to bind her in their tentacles.

'Aita, do you love all your seven children the same way? Or did your love for Dangor jethai decrease after the younger children were born?'

Her grandmother had spread out the sheath of a betel-nut tree as a mat and was peeling jackfruit seeds. She used the opportunity of an empty house to ask this question. Surprised to hear the usually silent girl speak, her grandmother tilted her head to look up at her.

'Not seven, my dear, I love all eight of them the same. The same as your mother loves you girls. When your khura was born, it was almost time to give the elder one away in marriage.'

'Who wanted to do that, Aita?'

'Your mastor koka, who else! She was barely twelve—she had just got to puberty when your grandfather arranged a match for her.'

She saw her grandmother sniffle and rub her nose.

'Including khura there are only seven, Aita . . . why are you saying eight?'

She finally got to the point.

With her head still bowed, her grandmother said, 'Oh . . . how do I say this. One of them crossed over to the other side. She used to look exactly like you.'

Realising that her mother would be returning soon, she wound up the discussion for the day. But she had finally got to know what everyone had tried to hide for so long—she used to have another aunt. But if she was no longer with them, then why didn't anyone ever show any sadness at losing her? There was not even an offering in the prayer room like on her grandfather's death anniversary. Her grandmother used to light an earthen lamp on the death anniversaries of her great grandparents.

* * *

Now forty, she was in charge of her own household. But she would still lapse into absentmindedness sometimes. Her grandmother had died the year she took her matriculation exams. Her father had found a groom for her after a year and sent her away. Just as the fish from the dead pukhuri were discarded, so too were her sisters thrown away to different homes as soon as they came of age. Afraid that they too might end up like his elder sister, their father had tied them down in marriage as soon as it was feasible. He had followed in the footsteps of his father. Their mother too perhaps sighed quietly now and then, like their grandmother, because their father had married them off too soon. She too was a fish from an interred pond whose voice had been silenced.

The pukhuri in the backyard had been filled up and a fresh one was dug nearby. The levelled-out old pukhuri now offered a clean and easy approach to the new one. A lemon plant occupied a pride of place in the centre of this area. The fragrance of the lemons permeated the air. Anyone could go there now; the elders no longer referred to the place as joiyal.

And they all ate the fish from the new pukhuri. Lemons and fish from the pukhuri were sent to the daughters' homes on Bihu and other special occasions. A dish prepared with the fish and the lemons was so tasty that people would lick their fingers long afterwards.

She would gaze at the fragrant lemon tree growing on the sacrifices demanded by tradition and people's egos. Yes, she had finally got to know the mystery of the joiyal pukhuri—she had managed to dig up the story frozen deep in the hearts of people. Though she had never even seen her innocent jethai, she felt sad at her fate.

The two elder jethais had been married off. They were hunting for grooms for the other two when her xoru jethai had eloped with a boy from the village without anyone having an inkling. Perhaps they took this step because they feared that the family would oppose their union. There was a furore at home. And the news spread like wildfire because it had happened in an important person's family. The young couple returned to his home after a week. The boy's family had no objection to her jethai. But her grandfather objected, for his reputation as a teacher lay tattered. He dragged his daughter to the cowshed and tied her up there. She was given food just once a day. This was her punishment for damaging mastor koka's reputation. And things continued this way for about a month, when it was discovered that she was pregnant. Before anyone else got to know about it, her grandfather summoned a midwife, and an abortion was induced at home. The crude operation, coming on top of malnutrition, made her body wither away till her bones poked out from her skin. One day, overcome with self-condemnation at damaging the family reputation and the disregard for her own aspirations, she took a decision. Now no one could eat any fish out of the pukhuri where they once used to literally jump out of the water. The incident stunned everyone. A diktat was laid down to ensure no other girl from the family ever committed the mistake of falling in love.

This was why she could never eat a fish from the pukhuri where they had buried her jethai. Nor could she suck on a lemon from a spot that had been used to trample upon young love so ruthlessly. She was sure her grandmother could not have done it either. For she too must have been a voiceless fish discarded from a dry pukhuri.

But even after she knew the whole story, she kept her silence. The knowledge of her young jethai being snuffed out made her miserable. And her silence strengthened her father's resolve even more. Love was always held up as an unnecessary and base emotion in their house. An image was created—the reputation of a family can only be upheld if there was no romance between young people. Like their jethai, they too wished to get acquainted with the word 'love'; but their father ensured that it was wiped out by the joyful, high-pitched sound of the urulis of the women welcoming the groom at their gate.

* * *

'O Ma . . . what are you thinking of, sitting here? Ryan wants to come home today, to meet you formally,' her daughter Ponkhi's voice dragged her back to reality.

'What . . .? Oh, Ryan . . .'

'Yes, Ma . . . Ryan. Didn't I tell you? Papa is more excited than you are about this.'

She paused for a moment on hearing her daughter speak so frankly. Ponkhi was back home for a few days after completing her medical studies. The pause jolted her—she hoped fervently that her father's ego had not made room for itself within her.

Amidst all her worries and anxieties, she had once made a promise to herself, 'I shall let my daughter be as free as a butterfly; let her be the master of her own pukhuri.' She had said the same thing to her husband too. She had poured out her heart out to him, telling him the story of the interred pukhuri. What he had said that day had filled her heart with affection. 'You too should fly, my love. You too should savour your own pukhuri.' And it was because of her nurturing that her daughter could now speak so frankly. All because of her.

'I'm so excited to meet your love, my dear,' she said in English. 'I was just thinking of the new recipes to try out when Ryan is here.'

THE ROAR OF BAGHJAN

Juri Baruah

Translated by Harsita Hiya

The night was like a deep forest grown old, except for the rumbling sounds from the oil field proudly declaring their dominance. Piercing the darkness, these sounds were like a rusty knife being twisted inside a wound. A sharp blade that spared no one. Not the fish in Maguri lake. Not the ruddy shelducks in the Motapung wetlands. Not even the pink lotuses blooming in the lake water.

Protik, who was about to take off his uniform, paused on hearing the sounds, his heart trembling. The spiralling smoke, heedless and reckless, had almost turned his uniform black. The silence, stillness and desolation of the outside world—drained by the strange heat—found an echo within him.

Covid-19 had arrived in the region even before they could recover from the floods, the lockdown weighing heavy on every household. In the middle of all this, there was the fire. Burning on for 150 days. Declaring itself invincible. It had spread from the oil fields, making its way into people's eyes. The company had now brought in Joseph, an Italian geologist, to tame it.

Protik craved a smoke after working several hours without a break, but it was no longer possible to light a cigarette on the site. The poisonous gases had filled the air already. He closed his eyes, brushing back the hair from his sweaty forehead. He wanted to forget the fearful gazes of the innocent villagers from the other side of the lake.

Half-asleep, Protik saw himself emerging from the oil field through a wall of ravenous flames. Joseph was in front of him, with Munin following behind.

Munin showed up in Protik's line of sight moments later, holding a first-aid box.

'Sir, you left this back at the site,' he said, holding it out for Protik.

Red eyes and burnt hands. Ash-covered hair and a black face. And yet, Munin hadn't forgotten to return Protik's first-aid box.

'Don't worry, Sir,' he said before leaving, 'Everything will be OK.'

'Everything will be OK'—Protik gave in to the assurance. A pointless, meaningless, senseless assurance.

Protik and Joseph often stood under the shed gazing at the oil field together. The things that Protik wanted to forget, to erase from every trace of time in those moments, were the very things Joseph wanted to carry back to his country.

As they stood there that day, Joseph took out a creased photograph from his wallet. It was the picture of a child. Golden-haired, hazel-eyed and white-skinned. He unfolded the picture, revealing a woman standing next to the child.

'This is Alice,' said Joseph in English, holding the photograph up for Protik, 'And the little one is Andrew.'

'Alice must have let the hens out by now,' he continued. 'And Andrew, he will be groping around inside the pen for eggs to deposit in his mother's lap. Alice will follow him into the kitchen yelling, and then cook sausages and eggs. I can almost see her sighing at the table, looking at the extra food, the portion meant for me she must have cooked out of habit.'

Joseph took a deep breath. Protik felt like a defeated general as he faced the unquenchable fire. Perhaps Joseph was beginning to feel the same way. It was why they were both looking at pictures of loved ones for comfort. The present was real. The fire too. Yet, so was the fervent hopefulness of living.

Life was truly a strange thing. Protik could catch a glimpse of it in Joseph's twinkling eyes. He had seen a similar glow in Munin's gaze. The same worldly light trapped between things lost and found.

Munin stood at a distance, eavesdropping on Joseph and Protik's conversation. He couldn't understand much of what they were talking about. The grief and tears in their words nonetheless felt all too familiar. People, it seemed, carried the same emptiness within despite being from different parts of the worlds. Munin couldn't help but think of Tora.

Protik had met her too. During a field visit to the other side of Maguri lake, Munin had convinced his boss to stop by his village and visit his home. Sitting on the long bench in their courtyard, Protik ran his eyes over Munin's house. In an instant, it became clear to him why Munin never shied away from any job on the site, be it serving betel leaf or lifting heavy pipes. Protik knew Munin wanted approval for his work. He wanted to be spoken of highly to their superiors. It was the only reason he had entirely forgotten the word 'No'.

Although betel leaves were not his favourite, that day Protik graciously accepted the tender betel nuts and leaves served by Munin's mother.

'It may make you dizzy, Sir,' she told him. 'Don't have it if you aren't used to it.'

Her artlessness made him stay back longer than he had planned to. Protik looked at his surroundings, imagining the blood and sweat Munin had poured into his home to keep it standing.

'You must eat with us before you go, Sir,' Munin's mother said to him, 'We are having duck today. Tora will be joining us.'

Munin looked uneasy. His house was hardly a place fit for his boss to eat in. He stood staring at Protik in silence.

'Thank you, but not today. I'm still on duty. I'll visit soon for lunch.'

With that Protik stood up to leave. The villagers gathered in the courtyard to see him off.

Fishing was the sole livelihood of the people who lived on this side of the lake, occasionally supplemented by small-scale farming. The income they made was enough to feed most of the families, though frugally. The people here didn't have huge godowns to fall back on. Thankfully, they didn't have long spells of shortages either. In the past, young men from almost every household of these villages had gone off to the rebel camps beyond the hills. Some of them had returned over time, managing to bag contracts with the oil company. The bodies of the others had never reached home. Yet, in spite of their hand-to-mouth existence, the villagers always cooked enough rice for an extra stomach, never letting guests return home unfed. Along with the foam of rice water, it was as if they had spent a lifetime skimming over all their worries and troubles.

A young woman was waiting at the far end of the courtyard.

'Sir, this is Tora. We are getting married this coming Aahin.'

Protik smiled at Tora. She seemed to be of Munin's age. She must have dressed up and rushed here on getting to know they had guests at the house.

'I'm afraid you will only have to cook for your fiancé today.'

Tora lowered her eyes, blushing.

The memory of their past encounter reminded Protik to ask Munin about her.

'Does she know the kind of things you have to do here?'

'She didn't before, but she has found out by now. The villagers talk, Sir.'

'Found out what? The risks?'

'Nothing like that, Sir. Every line of work has its own risks. That she understands. Besides, she's the one taking the biggest risk of them all by marrying me!'

Protik laughed out loud. Munin put on his helmet and walked into the rig. Joseph didn't understand what he said, but he knew all too well that pain was articulated the same way in every language. In the past few days, Joseph had realised that, even though the company had seemingly employed him to save the locals, his own security was their main concern. It was why they sent him new directives on a daily basis through Protik.

'Don't go anywhere alone, Joseph. I have just received orders from above.'

A lifetime of working in the heart of forests, deserts and poverty-riddled countries had taught Joseph an important lesson—corporations had more power over nations than their own governments.

'Guns, money and oil—seems we can't live without them,' he said suddenly.

Protik could decipher what he meant.

'You know, Joseph, if it hadn't been for the arrival of Italian engineers, oil would have perhaps never been discovered in our land.'

'Oh really?'

'In those days, tracks were being laid down from Margherita to Dibrugarh, overseen by the Assam Railway and Trading Company. Forests were being cleared. The unexpected appearance of oil bubbling within one such forest lit up the faces of the Italians. Supervising the construction of a railway line had led them to discover oil. Strange, isn't it?'

'Guns, money and oil,' Joseph reiterated. 'It's certainly hard to prove which is more powerful.'

Joseph paused. After a while, he said without looking at Protik, 'But we do have proof. Some of it was offered up to display power, while some of it was aimed at filling others with fear. The world abounds with the history of such proof, my friend.'

Joseph exuded confidence when he spoke. Perhaps this was how his experience had honed him.

'So . . . does the Front still hold any sway in these parts?

'Why do you ask?' Protik responded, 'Any abduction fantasies you want me to know about?'

Despite the tense atmosphere, the two laughed out loud.

The head office had briefed Joseph unofficially on certain matters before his trip here. They had informed him how many former foreign employees of the company had become the targets of the armed separatist front called ULFA.

'You know, Joseph,' said Protik, 'there's no clear answer to your question. I don't believe the Front alone turned anyone rebellious. Rebellion was already lurking in a corner of people's hearts. A pretext was all it needed to come up to the surface.'

Protik, Munin and Joseph today had no pretext—no luxury of a shortcut. The fire had raged on like a jilted lover, sneaking poisonous gases into the air. Sometimes it acted in the strangest manner, bubbling up from the earth, revealing every shade of its anger, exhaustion and torment. Then it exploded. Long after each explosion, it was easy for everyone around to believe in the fire.

Those who believed in fires nurtured flames in their own eyes. Joseph, Protik and Munin were among all the men who had ended up trying to tame these flames, ever since, seeking the answer to the same question—mankind may be hardy, but what about time?

Protik and Joseph returned to their seats for lunch. A

bleary-eyed Tora was waiting for Munin by the shed with a tiffin box.

'This foul wind has already reached the village,' she said, looking up at him.

'Which company can stop the wind, you tell me?'

'How can you still be siding with the company?'

'I'm not picking sides, I'm only doing my job.'

'Doing your job, but what about your judgement? Is that gone with the wind too?'

'Tora . . . you must stop coming here . . .'

Tora walked away. The tiffin box in Munin's hands grew colder the further she went. Although he was as strong as a bodybuilder, he found it difficult to lift each morsel of rice to his mouth, feeling something quivering inside his chest. He couldn't tell what it was. It was like a bird with broken wings collapsing on the ground. Like a loose elastic band falling from Tora's long tresses. Like a white frangipani drifting down quietly and brushing against his mother as she stood waiting for him by the gate. Like the deep, low voice of his elder brother, his mirror image, who had lost his way years ago.

Munin couldn't finish the lunch Tora had lovingly brought for him. Suddenly, another booming sound was heard across the site. Panic took over the workers, and Protik and Joseph rushed outside. The atmosphere became unbearable, thanks to the nameless gases in the air. Oil drops were falling like rain.

Protik, Munin and Joseph assembled in the shed. The colours in the sky over the other side of the lake ranged from a deep yellow to a fierce red, like the eyes of an angry tiger.

'You need to alert the people', Joseph said without looking at Protik.

For what seemed like ages, Protik kept gaping at Joseph. He eventually switched on his satellite phone. They would now have to evacuate all three villages on the other side of the lake overnight.

Munin felt as he could hear a flock of noisy vultures flying overhead.

Where were all the people supposed to go? And overnight, at that? Would they agree to leave behind their homes, everything? Would the company bear the responsibility for them?

His elder brother had once asked him the same question. Years ago, the family had lost a son to ULFA. Dangor da had left to join the Front, the one that told men to walk with guns in their hands and no fear in their hearts. This was the story Munin had heard throughout his youth.

The ULFA men had tried to intimidate the company— how could they build their rig on land owned by the villagers, and right next to the lake, at that?

'No guts to come back home, but look at him! Trying to threaten a company,' Munin's father would mutter every now and then.

Still, his mother had carried on cooking meals for four people, serving four portions of chicken curry seasoned with pepper, and fish steamed in banana leaves. Even after blowing out the lamp by the door for the last time, Aai had not closed her eyes.

Munin recalled it all. On bleak, hazy nights, people tend

to remember those they love. It was something no one had needed to teach him as a boy.

He returned to the present and looked at Protik.

'Sir, could I send a message home?'

For the first time, Protik could see doubt clouding Munin's eyes.

'Whom would you like to call?'

'Tora. She alone can convince my mother.'

Protik immediately handed over the satellite phone.

A milkwood tree had once stood at the site of the oil rig. It was where Munin and his friends had gathered to practice singing and dancing together for the Bihu festival before going door to door with their performances. It was beneath this tree that his old friend Tora had gifted him a gamusa as well as a first kiss. He could hardly believe that a fire was now ravaging the same place.

Munin summed up the situation for Tora as briefly as possible.

'Don't leave Aai alone.'

'And you?'

'Don't think too much about me, OK?'

'What do you mean? The hens have started dropping dead since yesterday. Mustard flowers have begun drooping and dying. So many people are complaining that they can't breathe.'

'Just . . . just don't think about me. Go wherever the company takes you. Please!'

A long sigh travelled across the ether, only to remain trapped between Tora and Munin. Munin exhaled, his breath answering the questions Tora could not ask. He hung up.

Years ago, after his father's death, Munin had made another phone call from a public phone booth in a similar state. The call had gone through only after several attempts. His throat had dried up at the sound of Dangor da's heavy voice on the other side.

'Pitai is gone,' he had whispered.

'I know.'

'Won't you come to see Aai once?'

'. . .'

Dangor da had fallen silent for a while.

'Why have the villagers allowed a lease on the land on our side of the lake? Will the company bear the responsibility for all of you if something goes wrong?'

'You're changing the subject, Dangor da.'

'Don't call back on this number, Moon. I'll make arrangements to send some money.'

Munin had found Dangor da selfish. He was deeply hurt and full of resentment. He wanted to scream out in fury that day, but not many things can be said in a one-rupee conversation.

He had kept sitting with the phone stuck to his ear long after ending the call. Tora must be doing the same now, he thought. She too must be frozen.

Those who stay frozen fear no fire. They have already been singed by the flames within.

The whole sky turned red on the final night. A sky roaring and rumbling like a tiger. Its colours were reflected dully in the lake, in the eyes of men like Munin, in the cacophony of a bird beating its wings to fly away, in the weeping of little children.

Protik ordered the evacuation of the site. By now, the fire had enveloped the surrounding vegetation and taken over the setup here. It was hard to keep track of anyone. Suddenly, Protik remembered he hadn't seen Joseph around.

'Munin, where is Joseph?' He asked.

Munin looked back. On a hunch, he began running towards the fire.

* * *

Protik was on his way back from the airport after seeing off Joseph. No matter how hard he tried not to think about it, the image captured by the drone on that fateful morning kept flashing before his eyes—the picture of a corpse floating towards him. That morning, that smell—was it the stench of the burnt oil or a burnt body?—still haunted his and Joseph's nights, robbing them of sleep.

Munin's mother would keep waiting to open the door. For many springs to come, Tora would feel no warmth within herself.

Protik suddenly turned his car to drive towards Munin's village. He hadn't been brave enough to attend the rituals performed on the third day after the cremation.

The long bench was lying as before in the courtyard of Munin's house. Munin's mother came outside on hearing the sound of the car. She was followed by Tora.

Protik looked at the old woman's quiet eyes and parched lips. Her clothes had as many wrinkles as her mind. His gaze turned to Tora as she brought out a tray of betel leaves and placed it in front of him. Protik picked up a tender betel nut with quivering hands.

'We are used to this, Sir,' Munin's mother whispered. 'To loss and suffering. To nurturing fires.'

Tora's eyes welled up, her nostrils flaring. She didn't say anything to Protik. This silence was no less than a scar. Enduring a fire hadn't become any easier.

ABOUT THE
AUTHORS AND TRANSLATORS

Harekrishna Deka (b. 1943) is considered to be one of the foremost Assamese writers today, known for his novel experiments in modern and postmodern Assamese literature during the last half century. He has a versatile pen and has distinguished himself in poetry, fiction and literary criticism. His fiction has broken new ground in both form and content. He has also been writing on various socio-political issues. Belonging to the Indian Police Service, he retired from service as the Director General of Police. After retirement, he briefly edited the Guwahati-based daily *The Sentinel* and then became the editor of the prestigious Assamese magazine *Goriyoshi* till his retirement. He has more than thirty books to his credit. Among the awards he has received are the Sahitya Akademi Award, the Katha Short Story Award, the Assam Valley Literary Award, in 2010, for his overall contribution to Assamese literature, and the Padmanatha Bidyabinod Literary Award, in 2015, for his contribution to Assamese poetry.

* * *

Imran Hussain (b. 1966) is an academician, writer and literary critic, a translator and lexicographer with four critically acclaimed works of fiction and short fiction. One of them, *Hudumdai Aru Ananyo Golpo*, was published by Sahitya Akademi. Other collections include *Rupantoror Gadya* and *Asthir Pranto*. Some of these stories have been performed as plays, including the 'The Water Spirit'. His works seamlessly blend folklore and myth with a deep compassion for the economically weaker sections of society, and rural citizens. His awards include the Katha Award for Creative Fiction and the Chandraprabha Memorial Award.

* * *

Purobi Bormudoi (1950–2019), a Sahitya Akademi awardee, was also the recipient of several other prestigious awards, such as the Prabina Saikia Award, Chhaganlal Jain Literary Award, and the Basanti Devi Award. Her works include a large number of short stories and novels. Some of her well-known works of longer fiction are *Santanukulanandan*, *Gajraj*, *Prem Aru Banditwa*, *Baghsaal*, *Baghjal Aru Manuh*, and *Rupowali Noi, Sonowali Ghat*. Her works are suffused with compassion for people as well as animals and a great deal of environmental awareness.

* * *

Mamoni Raisom Goswami (1942–2011), also known as Indira Goswami, is a Jnanpith awardee, a Sahitya Akademi awardee, and a noted Ramayan scholar whose work was recognized and lauded worldwide. She was an academic, novelist and short story writer whose fictional works are imbued with compassion, a sense of history, and anger against social injustices and inhuman practices against both men and women. Though awarded a Padma Shri, she declined the award. She was also the recipient of the Principal Prince Claus Laureate Award of the Netherlands, the monetary component of which she donated to charitable causes. Among the numerous awards she received were the Kamal Kumari Award, the Mahiyoshi Joymoti Award, the Katha National Award, honorary D Litt degree from Rabindra Bharati University, West Bengal, and other universities, the International Tulsi Award, and also the highest civilian award of the Government of Assam, the Assam Ratna. She was also an activist, and a mediator between the armed militant group United Liberation Front of Assam and the Government of India. Her popular novels are *Chenabor Srot* (The Chenab's Current) *Neelkanthi Braja* (The Blue-Necked God), *Mamore Dhora Torowal* (The Rusted Sword), *Dontal Hatir Uiyey Khowa Howdah* (The Termite Ridden Howdah of the Tusker), *Tej aru Dhulirey Dhuxorito Prishtha* (Pages Stained with Blood and Dust), *Thengphakhri Tehsildaror Tamor Tarowal* (The Bronze Sword of Thengphakhri Tehsildar) as also several collections of short stories and autobiographical works.

* * *

Gayatri Bhattacharyya worked in St Edmund's College, Shillong, before joining Gauhati University. After retirement, she took up translation as a hobby, and has since translated many anthologies of short stories and novels written by eminent Assamese writers into English, including works by Sarat Chandra Goswami, Bhabendra Nath Saikia, Mamoni Roisom Goswami, Anuradha Sarma Pujari, Dipak Barkakati, and Birinchi Kumar Barua. So far she has fifteen books to her credit, besides many short stories and articles, published in anthologies and newspapers.

* * *

Mitali Goswami is a critic, translator and educator. Her recent works include chapters in *How to Tell the Story of an Insurgency*, *Female Author-ity*, and the very well-received book titled *The Water Spirit and Other Stories*.

* * *

Madhurima Baruah Sen, born in 1961, did her M.A. in Economics, Dibrugarh University, Assam and Master of Planning, School of Planning and Architecture, New Delhi. Although now retired, she was selected for the Assam Civil Services as a Class I officer in 1986 and worked at the Indian Administrative Services as the Secretary of the Cultural Affairs Department. Her personal essays were published in different newspapers and later compiled as *Jiwanar Dukhariya Chabi*. She translated Dale Carnegie's books into Assamese. She was selected as a jury member for the International Film Festivals in Barcelona (2018), Poland (2019) and Nepal (2021).

* * *

Syeda Shaheen Jeenat Suhailey is a reader first and a writer later, as she shares her family's love for books. Her hobbies include sampling different cuisines and listening to music. She has written over 300 poems with nearly sixty published in English dailies and magazines and started translating recently with hopes of translating the works of legendary Assamese writers like Bhabendra Nath Saikia and Syed Abdul Malik among others. An alumnus of the Tezpur University, she did her M.A. in Mass Communication and Journalism in 2012. She has written sporadically through the years, both fiction and nonfiction. Currently, she works as an online content creator and lives with her parents.

* * *

Ashamoni Neog, pursuing her PhD in Physics at Tezpur University, Assam, harbours a keen interest for books, movies, music, art and photography. She feels greatly influenced by English and French literature, and other literary translations. Being inspired by old Hindi songs, she indulges in singing and composing music, too. Her love for sci-fi and thriller movies nudged her towards acting. She directed and produced a short film named 'In Search of Clean Water' under SCoPE-Assamese, administered by the department of Journalism and Mass Communication at Tezpur University. She hopes to work towards the welfare of the society and make scientific innovations in future, like Elon Musk.

* * *

Niruja Bora is working to develop micro-stories in Assam. She had started a Facebook group named 'Anugalpo' in 2018 which garnered a lot of recognition, resulting in the page being tied to almost 72,000 readers and writers currently. She has been awarded the Lekhok Sambardhana Award by the Government of Assam and the Avishek Award by Rahasya Prakashan of Assam. She has also authored a short-story book called *Bowati Kalangar Senduriya Chabi* and edited a book called *Anugalpo Samahar*.

* * *

Nilutpal Baruah, born in 1982, published his first book *Bandhya Prahoror Kobita* in 1999. Baruah was an executive editor for the newspaper *Axomiya Natyosinta*. Baruah was awarded the Mamoni Roisom Goswami Memorial Award for his novel *Indraprasthat Priyodarshini*. He produced seven documentary films about the theatre and folk culture in Assam and has been involved with Assamese music as a lyricist for a decade. Baruah was awarded the Kala Guru Bishnu Prasad Rabha Award and the Sahitya Botafor his book *Sukracharjya Rabha, Jatra Aru Matra*, which was translated into English as *Sal Soul Sukracharjya*. Currently, he is working on a collection of short-stories and a novel.

* * *

Rashmi Baruah did her M.A. in Mass Communication, Jamia Millia Islamia, New Delhi, and B.A. in English, Cotton College, Guwahati. She worked at *The Assam*

Tribune, made documentaries for DD North-East and worked on 'Surviving with a Smile', a documentary on a cancer survivor. She wrote a column, 'Delhir Diary', for *Asom Bani*, an Assamese weekly; did various translation works and won the first prize in an all-India translation competition. She was a cameraperson and news anchor at BiTv (TVI), directed 'The Golf Show' for Ten Sports and 'Bridging Giants', a series for Singapore TV. She anchored shows, news and sports events like Commonwealth Games, Asian Games and Afro—Asian Games.

* * *

Juri Baruah is a storyteller by passion and geographer by profession. She is a follower of Marxist feminism. She was the Editor of the *Cottonian* magazine in 2010–11. Her first short-story collection, published in 2016 and republished in 2020, is recognised widely. Her second short-story collection *Prakton* was published in 2022. Her stories have been translated into English, Bengali and Hindi. She believes that stories are real rather than imaginary. Currently, she is working on a novel.

* * *

Manaswinee Mahanta is an Assistant Professor in the School of Communications and Media at the Assam Royal Global University, Guwahati. She is a researcher in the field of film and society. She is pursuing her PhD from Tezpur University, a Central University in the state of Assam. A documentary film maker and script-writer, Mahanta has written screenplay and scripts for films and theatres. She has also been working extensively in the field of folk and traditional theatre, believing in the capacity of people's theatre to evoke changes in society.

* * *

Jintu Gitartha, real name Jintu Thakuria, is a short-story writer also involved in translation. Having graduated in Education from Cotton University and in Assamese from KKHSOU, he is currently pursuing an M.A. in Education at Cotton University. His short stories have been published in leading Assamese journals. He authored a short-story collection 'Sabir Vram, Vramar Sabi' and co-authored *Sikshar Mahan Chintabidsakal*, *Manasik Swasthya Aru Swasthya Vijnan*, *Jeevan Tathya Lakhan aru Sakhyatkar Pradan*. He has won the Bhasha Gaurav Award, Young Researcher Award and Jogananda Borgohain Memorial Award for his short story 'Sajbela-Kalbela'. His short story 'Magur' is adapted from 'The Catfish', a short film screened at various national and international film festivals.

* * *

Harsita Hiya is a writer, translator and short fiction lover hailing from the town of Nagaon, Assam. An English postgraduate from Jawaharlal Nehru University, Delhi (2017–19), and a graduate from Ramjas College, University of Delhi (2014–17), she was one of the three winning authors in the Storyteller Contest organised by Tweak India. *Grandmother's Tales*, her English translation of Lakshminath Bezbaruah's *Burhi Aair Xadhu* was published by Akhar Prakash in December 2020. Her work has previously been featured in *Muse India* and *The Little Journal of North East India*.

* * *

Binu Das, born 1966, is a children's fiction author and subject teacher of Assamese at Changsari HS School. She completed her M.A. in Assamese from Gauhati University in 1992 and worked in print media before taking up a teaching job. She has published a collection of children's short stories called *Picnic* (Chandra Prakash, 1998). Her writing has appeared in various newspapers and magazines, most notably her story 'Utkanthar Antat', in *Prantik*. She is currently working on her first novel, which looks at climate change through the perspective of children, in her hometown Guwahati.

* * *

Bikash Dihingia, birth name Budhidipta Dihingia, lives in Dhulpeta Gaon, Assam. Being a shy child, he found solace in the river near his house. He enjoys trekking, adventure and photography. His father Sri Lakhi Dihingia and mother Srimati Anita Dihingia are his biggest supporters. He has been writing for a children's magazine, *Mouchaq*, since primary school. With a degree in Science from Dhakuakhana College and a Diploma in Elementary Education from DIET, Lakhimpur, he was selected under the Ministry of Education's PM YUVA Mentorship Scheme, among seventy-five authors. Unaware of his real name until the HSLC exam, he continues to use his pen name, unable to adjust to his birth name.

* * *

Debasish Buragohain, a twenty-three-year-old author born in Ghilamara, Assam, and currently residing in Tezpur, is a keen learner of all the genres of literature. With a bachelor's degree from North Lakhimpur College, he is studying for an M.A. in Assamese from Tezpur University. He has been an editor in various magazines. His short stories and poems have been broadcast on All India Radio, Dibrugarh, and two poems have been published in *Satsori*, a literary magazine in Assàm. He has won over twenty state-level competitions, represented his institution in state-level quiz competitions and is the editor of the first issue of *Kixalaya*, an e-magazine of the department of Assamese, Tezpur University.

AFTERWORD

The writers published in *A Fistful of Moonlight* came together through the Write Assamese project, in response to research by the British Council showing that the translation ecosystem in India suffers from a lack of training opportunities. In addition, aspiring fiction writers are often marginalised with little chance of developing their work in the absence of a publishing infrastructure for the 22 official and 700 spoken languages in the country.

The Northeast of India consisted of the seven contiguous states of Arunachal Pradesh, Assam, Meghalaya, Manipur, Mizoram, Nagaland and Tripura and now with the inclusion of the state of Sikkim, this has risen to eight. Although geographically close, they remain culturally distinct. Assam is the largest state, with a primarily Assamese-speaking population, and outside of India is probably best known for its tea, wildlife, and weaving – it has the largest population of weavers in India. It also bears the scars of many years of unrest. Since the 1970s, separatist and insurgent groups have been at odds with the Indian Government over political, social, cultural and economic issues, and increased levels of illegal immigration from Bangladesh. This has exacerbated the challenges for a local creative infrastructure to establish itself and has left many aspiring writers with few opportunities to share their work with experienced literary editors, particularly in translation.

It was against this backdrop that the British Council invited Untold Narratives, based in London, to replicate the editorial model used in its Write Afghanistan project – that of literary translator, editor and writer working closely together throughout the editorial development process. In Afghanistan the process was delivered remotely; for Write Assamese, the British Council approached BEE Books, an independent press based in Kolkata. BEE comes from a long history of Bengali publishing and has, in the last eight years, carved out a place for itself as a publisher of translated works, with a wide range of titles from different Indian and international languages. Untold partnered with BEE Books to deliver an eight-day long editorial workshop focussed on fostering consistent, quality translations to generate new Assamese fiction for international audiences.

In the spring of 2022, the partners issued an 'open call' on social media and local radio across Assam to attract new, unpublished stories in Assamese by emerging writers. Writers across the state, aged 18 and over, were invited to submit short pieces of fiction to be considered for the project. The call attracted 83 submissions from 16 translators and 67 writers.

A team of local readers and editors sifted these submissions, and after the preliminary sorting, the project's local mentors, Arunava Sinha and Mitra Phukan, identified three translators and the ten stories with the greatest potential for publication, locally, nationally and globally. The resulting group included emerging writers aged between 18 and 63.

As the Assamese editor, Mitra Phukan, mentions in her

foreword to *A Fistful of Moonlight*, the subsequent editorial workshop process was new to many of the participants. Writers, editors and translators gathered in Kaziranga National Park to discuss and re-draft these stories for publication in both Assamese and separately in English for a wider readership. New creative relationships were forged. Three of the stories – 'Roots', 'Boots', and 'The Wagtail's Song' – have been taken up and published in Words Without Borders (December 2022).

The range of pieces in *A Fistful of Moonlight* reflects the diversity of writers involved in the project – some are from remote areas, like Majuli, Nagaon, Shivsagar, while others from towns and cities across the state. All, in their own way, reflect the writers' concerns, and their commitment to the region. An additional four stories edited and selected by Mitra Phukan have been included to broaden the context of this collection and to enable these ten emerging writers to sit alongside more established Assamese voices.

Along with support from KfW Stiftung in Germany, *A Fistful of Moonlight* is published as part of the British Council's India/UK Together season marking the 75th anniversary of modern India and highlighting the friendship and cultural bonds between the two countries, while also addressing shared global challenges. Write Assamese is a model and a catalyst for this developing relationship.

London, India
November 2022

Lucy Hannah
Director, Untold Narratives CIC

Esha Chatterjee
CEO and Founder, BEE Books

PROJECT PARTNERS

Untold Narratives CIC develops and amplifies the work of writers marginalised by community or conflict. Its editors and translators work collaboratively with writers to develop their craft, connect them to one another, and share their stories with new audiences in translation. Website link: *https://untold-narratives.org/*

BEE Books, the publisher of this collection in India, started its journey in 2014 with the primary area of focus in contemporary fiction, non-fiction, innovative illustrated titles and translations in the English language. Its roots go back to Patra Bharati, the third largest Bengali publishing house in India with a repertoire of 2000 titles of varied genre. Being a part of a regional market, the house realises the magnitude of Indian literature and the importance of bringing it to the fore. Website link: *www.beebooks.in*

The stories in *A Fistful of Moonlight* were developed through the Write Assamese project, a collaboration between Untold Narratives and BEE Books.

British Council is the UK's international organisation for cultural relations and educational opportunities.

The Council supports peace and prosperity by building connections, understanding and trust between people in the UK and countries worldwide. This is achieved through arts and culture, education and the English language. India/UK Together, a Season of Culture, marks the deep connections and 75th anniversary of India with a landmark programme that strengthens the friendship and vibrant cultural bonds of both countries, while addressing shared global challenges.

KfW Stiftung is an independent, non-profit foundation established in 2012 and based in Frankfurt am Main, Germany. Its activities include the promotion of cultural diversity across arts and culture, as well as engagement in responsible entrepreneurship, society and ecology. KfW Stiftung collaborates with partner organisations to strengthen creativity, freedom of expression and discussion and to create new platforms for the international contemporary arts. In collaboration with Untold, KfW Stiftung develops and promotes new literary voices.